# Lipstick, Fedora

## Shortstories X6

*By Jason and Viva Gabbard*

# Contents

Margaret ................................................................. 5

The Dishwasher ........................................................ 13

Wide Awake ............................................................ 30

The Fishing Trip ....................................................... 40

Lipstick, Fedora ....................................................... 88

The Documentary ..................................................... 110

# Margaret

I worked in a local bar when I was younger. There were many regulars, but one customer stands out in my mind. Margaret was what we called, in those days, a "bag lady". She slept in the alley behind the bar. All of her earthly belongings were in a shopping cart that she had found somewhere. She collected bottles and cans for money. As soon as I started working there, the owner of the bar told me that we were to look after her. "Whatever she wants", he said. "Take good care of her. Everything is on the house." I thought this was an odd request, but I was happy to follow it. She came in each night about an hour before closing time, never wanting more than a few shots of Jack and an audience. I believe she was mentally ill, as she rarely addressed anyone directly. When she did, it was something off-color or of a sexual nature. What was most striking

5

about Margaret was how she communicated with people through a set of hand puppets. She fabricated the puppets out of bits of trash and found objects that she collected. I had seen her on a number of occasions on the sidewalk, rocking back and forth, talking to herself while she made them. There were pieces of plastic, hair she had pulled from a hairbrush, and paper and fabric which were delicately cut to make clothes and accessories. The detail in the design of the puppets was remarkable. She had some savant-type talent, as each puppet was made in the likeness of people she saw on the street and was a work of art in and of itself. When she used them to communicate, you almost forgot that Margaret was there and, as strange as this sounds, became engaged in talking to the puppets.

The weather had changed for the worse one evening and I was out back finishing off half a spliff that I had in my shirt pocket. As I lit up, I noticed Margaret huddled under a shelter made of cardboard boxes and a tarp.

"That's quite a pad you got there, Margaret. Is that gonna keep you dry?"

"In my younger days, I could pop your cork off in a jiffy, if you know what I mean," was her reply.

"Well, isn't that nice." I didn't know what else to say. She was as old as my grandmother, maybe older. I couldn't help but visualize her doing that to someone. I shook my head to erase the image and handed her what was left of the smoke.

"Do you wanna come inside a little early and warm up? You can at least stay dry."

On her right hand was a puppet that now came to life. Exquisitely designed, it was a young woman with her hair neatly twisted into bun on her head and a Victorian style dress.

"I think I like him," Margaret spoke in the puppet's voice. The puppet looked at me. Margaret looked at the puppet.The puppet whispered to Margaret's ear.

"Yeah, yeah. I think that's him." Margaret stared at me with blank eyes as she listened to the puppet and nodded her head.

They conversed for a moment, then Margaret took a drag from the spliff.

"OK. I'll come in." It was as if another person had taken her over. She spoke directly to me and as lucidly as I had ever heard her speak to anyone.

The night went on like most other nights. Fifteen minutes before closing, Margaret sat at the bar. I flashed the lights on and off and gave last call. It was a slow night but there were a few orders - a glass of Cabernet, scotch and water, and a Screwdriver. Margaret ordered her usual three shots of Jack Daniels. She lifted the glass, made a salute to me, and threw it back. She slammed the glass down on the bar and smiled at me. I finished my side work for the night. When the clock hit 2:00am, I ushered everyone out and locked the door. I walked to the bar where Margaret sat.

"I want to tell you a story," she said.

I nodded. I wasn't in a hurry to get out in the rain. The weather had turned to crap and I was going to enjoy the warmth of the bar before walking home.

Margaret put a puppet on each hand. The one on her right was the woman from before. Her features were sharp, but she had a warm smile painted on her face. On her left was a man who resembled *me.* He was young, his hair was black like mine, and it appeared to be made from a piece of para-cord that had been meticulously unwound and combed out.

"Margaret, I have to say that you have an amazing talent for making puppets. They are true works of art."

"Thank you," she said. "Everything can be recycled. I make them from stuff that people put in the trash. I don't have to buy materials, people throw away all of this stuff. I learned how to sew when I was young." Then, her eyes glazed over and she was lost in the memory. Slowly the puppets began to move as if they were just waking up. Margaret began a narration.

"Just a life time ago, there were two people who had lived together before, and again before that. They were companion souls that have a standing agreement to meet and part and meet again."

She then began a dialogue. Margaret was the voice for both puppets, but in her hands the scene came to life. I became more and more involved with the story. It was how she manipulated the puppets - they became real on her hands, the way she moved them was expressive and spoke directly of their experience. No longer in the bar, I had been transported to the early American West. The man and woman had grown up in the same village in Austria. They had run away and migrated to America because there was too much bad blood between their families; therefore, marriage was impossible. Arriving in the new country, they married and settled on some promising river bottom land in Texas. He was a smart young man, a saddle maker by trade and had developed a strong business. Each day was a testament to their love. They spent time together every day, working the land and simply being in each others' company. I began to see myself in the story. I developed a real sense of the man, how he felt, and what he experienced. Oddly, I began to see Margaret as the woman in the story. I wanted to know what it all meant. He was to take a train to New York to make a saddle for a famous race horse. Both of them knew in their hearts this would be their last parting; at the station, they embraced. They each spoke of their eternal love for the other. They looked into each other eyes...

Suddenly, there was flash of lightning and thunder that startled me out of the trance. I was leaning on the bar with my chin resting in my hands. The puppets were embracing between us, as if about to kiss.

"Margaret, what happened at the station?"

She grabbed each side of my head with a puppeted hand. She pulled my face toward hers and we kissed passionately. I saw her as the woman from the story, the woman whom the puppet represented. I felt in her spirit a complete, unconditional love. I had the realization that the lives with which we identify can be recycled and re-lived, with the full memory thinly veiled beneath our consciousness. I wanted her. I opened my mouth to kiss her. As my tongue slid into her mouth, I brushed against her only front tooth - it had a rough, un-brushed texture and it was sharp on one corner. Her breath tasted of whiskey and sardines. I was suddenly jolted back to reality. I pushed away from the bar, and from her.

"What the...? Are you some kind of witch?

"No, my love, we *both* agreed it would be different this time. I've been waiting for you."  She threw back the remaining two shots, one after the other, and threw the glasses on the floor. She laughed insanely and ran out into the night. I never saw Margaret again. After several years, changes of jobs,  and a different town,  I received a letter from a lawyer in regard to a probated will. Thinking it was a scam, I tossed the letter into the recycling bin.  After two or three more notices and a nudging from my then-fiancée, I gave the law firm a call. It turned out that Margaret had passed away and she was the heiress to a fortune worth many millions of dollars. Her estate was to be split between myself and the bar owner who had shown her so much kindness. In the blink of an eye, my whole world changed. My fiancée and I were married and we've chosen to use the money to help others by setting up a foundation and a non-profit to help the homeless. We are having amazing experiences and now our greatest adventure is due any day – a baby girl to be named Margaret.

# The Dishwasher

I was staring into a pot of dishwater when it all started to make sense.

The water was tepid by now and the soap beginning to dilute. The layer of bubbles suddenly looked like a galaxy. A spiraling mass, groups of matter; some moving toward each other, some moving apart. Some were amassed in larger systems of swirls, like hurricanes in the galactic ocean. All moving in perfect, chaotic orchestration around a center that was moving and changing shape.

Gravity. It's the root cause. Motion. The universe is always moving, coming into order and moving into disarray. Like a big breath, in and out.

Dishes were always a zen-like action for me. They're like brushing your teeth or making your bed.

I'd been doing a lot of dishes lately. I mean, "chop wood, carry water", right? The dishes must be done.

Sometimes we can find enlightenment in the most mundane, common experiences. My experience was working in a kitchen as the dishwasher. I'm Cliff Lollard and I am some sort of "universal accident." Right now, this is who I am. Twenty-two, struggling, and trying to find my place in life.

As soon as the realization came, I put the couch out in the front yard. I don't really know why, but it seemed like the thing to do at the time. I'd been looking for my true voice. I don't know if I ever had any original thoughts. Do we come here preprogrammed? What to say? How to react? Grudges to bear? Where did all those things come from? Still looking for a voice that sounds like mine, then it comes like a flash. *They are not. You, Cliff, are special. Among all humans to be on earth at this time, you are like the galactic transistor radio. Tuning in to all the latest and breaking news. Whether you are able to keep your feet on the ground or not.*

The neighbors seem to take everything in stride. As I sat there, trying to get a grip on all the thoughts bouncing around inside my head, they waved on their way to wherever.

I guess my actions were beginning to attract attention. It was misting on the morning that the cops showed up. I don't know how long I had been sitting out on the couch in the yard, but I saw the sky light up as the sun rose somewhere beyond the heavy greyness.

"Is everything okay here, sir?" a younger officer asked. "Do you need help with anything?" asked the other, paunchier cop.

"No. I'm okay," I said.

"Is this your house?"

"Yes."

"Why are you sitting out here, on a couch in the front yard, in the... rain?"

"It clears my head," I said.

"Well, okay," said the paunchy cop.

He was looking more and more swine-like as he stood there with his hands on his hips, staring at me with his "I'm in charge here" look on his face. I could feel - or see, I don't know which - that he was assessing me, wondering what kinda dope I'd been smoking and when was he going to get to stuff and cuff me.

*You skinny little piece-of-shit hippie dope fiend. I'd love to give you a dose of reality with my asp. Just one or two whacks on the side of the head. Fucker.*

Those were his exact thoughts, but he was playing it cool.

"We're gonna need to see some I.D.," he said a little more sternly.

"Yes, sir," I said, "my wallet is in my left back pocket." I lifted my hands to show submission. "Is it okay if I reach back and get it out?"

"This hop-head is gonna be a wise guy!" said Officer Swine.

"Look... I'm not on any drugs, okay? I'm a spiritual trance channeler. I've been experiencing some revelations lately and I sit out here to ground myself. Is there an ordinance against doing this?"

"Well, you see sir," the younger one started, "there is an ordinance about having a couch in your front yar-"

"That's it!" shouted the piggish cop.

Immediately came the flash, then the noise. To describe it is hard, but if you've ever seen Jimi Hendrix at the Monterrey Pop Festival when he sets his Stratocaster on fire and hits it on the ground for about the fifth or sixth time... Well, that's the sound it made. Then everything went dark.

It was kind of like the time I was changing out wall sockets in the back bedroom. I had done all of the necessary steps to ensure that I would not be shocked. I did not account for a surge in the power grid. It hit the breaker box and jumped across all the switches at the precise moment I was touching a brass screw with a substandard flat head screwdriver and BZZZZZZ. That vibrating sense of joy and pain that electricity causes. It was similar to that.

Then comes the roller coaster ride where you realize that there is no track past the second turn and you just started your 200ft decent to build up enough inertia to pull the G's to get you there. You scream as you try to get back in control. Then it explodes out the bottom of your feet and you become a conduit of the Luminous Blue Energy that flows in your head and out to the ground, then permeates everything.

"Ooooh. Wow!? Did you fall down?" Christina was always inquisitive. "We've missed you around here. Everyone here at the cafe has had to take our turn to keep your job for you. You owe us all."

"Thanks," I said.

But the few weeks that had passed were a blur. I remembered the hospital, some. Vague glimpses of the ambulance in my front yard. My head, still very swollen. The bruising around my eye was a sunset mix of grape, yellow, and green, and my mental acuity was still very, very dull.

"No, I didn't fall down," I forced out.

I never mentioned that the cops had been there and neither did anyone else. She was one of the few people who either understood me, or was apathetic enough not to pry into my life. I felt the same about her, so I never questioned, for instance, her choice of attire, like why she wore a belt all the time with a buckle that spelled the name "Jesus."

It was no use - I couldn't explain much of it, nor would anyone probably understand fully. I don't. I had, since I met her, had an affinity for her that I could not shake. She was one of those rare creatures. She could never belong to anyone. She was beautiful and smart and was not to be tamed, like a feral horse with the spirit of the wind. Not to insinuate that she was promiscuous, but that her capacity for life and adventure was bigger than all of us in her immediate surroundings. It was good to be back at work.

"Hey, I've got to go," she said. "I'd tell you to give me a call sometime, but I can't find my phone."

"It's between the wall and your bed," I answered back.

I don't know how or why I knew. Just one of those quirks of my 'gifts'. I could locate almost anything that was lost, as long as it was of no direct benefit to myself. In other words, I could find other people's stuff just by knowing, but I often misplaced my own things, never to see them again.

"Okay," she said with an amused tone. "I'll look there."

Then she left. This wasn't the first time I had located something for her, but it still struck people oddly sometimes.

I was gathering the kitchen hardware to start the evening washing. I was usually there after everyone had left, cleaning up what was left over from that night. I enjoyed the solitude. It helped me to think. I was just getting lost in a pot of soapy warm water when my phone rang and snapped me back to the kitchen. It was my dad.

"Hey son, I've got to tell you that your Aunt Constance is in the hospital. It's not looking good. Can you make it a point to come down and see her?"

"I'll see what I can do," I said. I went back to

washing the dishes.

My Aunt Constance had lived a full life. She drank, she smoked, and she had a good time. She was my favorite Aunt. I had to go see her.

I took a taxi to the hospital. When I arrived, she was sleeping. She looked small there, in the bed, with tubes in her nose to help her breathe and a morphine drip in her hand to ease the pain. I reached down to touch her head and then the jolt came. A strange thing - my gift, if you want to call it that. I never know when or how it is going to manifest.

As I touched her, I suddenly and instantly became aware of every fun thing she had ever done. Everything. Every giggle and smile. Every birthday party. Every urge to have sex. The birth of her children. Every breath, from infant to adult. My 'gift' does not discriminate; I also became aware of the down sides too. Every time she went to the bathroom. Every wasted night that ended in shame. Every abusive relationship, every illness. Life is measured in breaths and heartbeats; I had become acutely aware of every single one, good or bad. I was aware of things that I shouldn't have been or didn't even really want to know. Deep secrets that were only known to her. I now shared that with her, like a lifetime of confession.

I came back to the room slowly. She was still sleeping but had a faint smile on her face. I kissed her and told her I loved her.

"Stay with me," I thought I heard her whisper.

Her eyes never opened again.

I needed to get grounded, so I left. She died that night in the hospital, hooked up to machines, high on morphine, and alone.

*Maybe next time*, I thought. *Maybe next time.*

Concentrations of mass slowly gravitate toward each other. As their mass and gravitation increases, they collapse upon themselves and begin to burn under their own weight and heat.

I was working on the garden in my back yard. It wasn't big, but I had the basics: squash, onions, potatoes, and a few herbs. I find that playing in the dirt gives me a sense of cleansing. With everything that was going on, now more than ever, I was isolating myself from the world. I was preparing for the "next season's growth". At least, that was what I was saying to myself.

I found a group of bug eggs under a cilantro shoot and brushed the silky, fuzzy encasement with the index finger of my left hand. The awareness of insect sight came into my inner vision. As I looked around in the shaded, filtered light of the insect's eye, I noticed that objects had a primal marking of luminescence that were in the frequencies of the spectrum. The plants, the animals.

A black grackle flew by and I saw in its feathers a pattern that I had never seen before, as if this faint light was some type of universal bar code for what that object was. The markings clearly stated to me, *I am hungry and horny. Do I want to eat you, fuck you, or flee from you? Did you notice that I have a beautiful beak? It is great for preening and catching flying things in the air that are smaller and slower than me.*

I heard someone knocking on the gate. I walked over, grabbed the powder-coated, well-used gate hardware, and swung it open. Christina was standing there in front of me. She looked radiant and more attractive than I had ever seen her before. Then it hit me, 'Wow! On the universal level, we all look like different forms of human-sized Comb jellyfish and we are all constantly advertising our thoughts, state of mind, and intentions to the world by strobing colors and patterns that speak directly to the subconscious.'

Her luminescent markings were so mesmerizing to

me that I must have looked rather dull, standing there, taking her in, and almost drooling on myself. They stated quite clearly and beautifully, *Hey, are you OK? You look kind of strange to me. You haven't been around lately, and I suddenly realized that I missed you. I don't know if I want to eat you, fuck you, or flee from you. Did you notice how well my body appears to be structured for having sex? It's great for catching things that are bigger, more physically powerful, and less cunning than me. I was curious as to why we have never 'hung out'.*

I can't imagine what my lights were saying.

*I also wanted to tell you about this article I found about the rare Coastal Cilantro Moth. They say that it has an invisible bio-luminescent pattern that is used to attract potential mates. I've heard you talk about them before. I thought you would be interested.*

Then, she shifted her weight from her right to left hip, which is almost imperceptibly subtle and can only be delivered with such mastery by a woman.

I asked her to come into the backyard. I told her I was feeling a little "uncentered" and I needed some time to get my feet on the ground.

She said, "No rush."

She came in and sat down in a lawn chair. I sat next to her and we just stayed that way for a while and looked at the scenery. I soon started to see and feel like myself again.

"So," I said, "you remembered about the cilantro moths?"

I didn't know what else to say. In my "normal" state, I felt awkward and unsure of what I thought was happening between us. She looked straight at me and said, "I'm trying to find balance. Do you know how someone can create balance in their lives?"

"Well," I said, "The masters say you have to start with your breath. You have to find your breath. I am trying to find my true voice, so I guess we're kind of looking for the same thing."

Our eyes found one another's and we were locked there for some timeless sequence. We were falling in toward each other like a magnet had been placed between us and neither could nor wanted to resist as our souls seemed to be reaching for each other.

Then I broke the spell. "I have to tell you that, if you touch me, or I touch you, or if we... well... I may have access to information about you that you may not want me to know. I want what I think is happening to happen, but I should warn you. This may get weird."

"Stand up," she said.

I stood and faced her, she faced me, and she grabbed both of my hands. "I'm not afraid," she looked right into my eyes.

The room started to blur at the edges of my vision and a shadow seemed to be circling the room as it grew darker and darker around us. She moved closer and kissed me on the mouth.

The universe is layered like an onion - more correctly, it should be described as a "multiverse" and is more shaped like a vase lying on its side. As vision becomes clear, the layer upon layer of parallels become apparent, like an echo of different variations reverberating ad infinitum.

An infinite video feedback loop of ourselves trailed out behind us. It was us, holding hands and kissing, but not us, as many manifestations of our lives together came into view at once and the space between them spanned eons, years, seconds, worlds, species. We were on two separate orbits that, from time to time, synched up and we traveled together until the arch of our paths pulled us away. At this point, we weren't aware of the other until we appeared as a faint star in each other's sky, growing brighter with remembrance only to join hands for a lifetime and then move on again.

This repeated itself hundreds of times. We both started crying uncontrollably with joy.

We hugged.

A star such as our sun gives off an unimaginable amount of energy.

Our bodies yearned to be joined together; we began taking off our clothes. When we came together again, she slid me into her. I felt the energy flood, into the top of my head, with an intensely white light. It flowed down my body and out of my penis. I could feel the energy rise in her body and re-enter me where our foreheads were touching. We were being swept away in the universal flow of yin and yang; it was all-consuming.

The flow was getting more and more intense and I was becoming afraid. She, on the other hand, was more active; there was a strange look in her eye.

She pushed me down on the floor and she was riding me and riding me. I could not tell if I was in danger of being injured or not. She was getting out of hand with it, and the wilder she got, the more the energy flowed.

I was about to climax out of sheer terror and pleasure. She could feel the energy growing too; she growled at me and then ground down harder.

Suddenly, with the reflexes of a cat, she sprung off of me and grabbed for her clothes. I was so shocked and stunned by her movement, and the sudden disconnection of the sexual energy, that I just lay there unable to move.

She slid the belt out of her pants and brandished it like an expert equestrian.

There was a loud smack.

Then, the stinging and the bleeding of a wound between skin and shallow bone. She hit me precisely on the ridge on the side of my head.

I shouted. "What the fuck!?" about a millisecond before the second one hit me on my left butt cheek, each following in rapid succession like an automatic rifle.

She hit me over and over and over. I became unconscious as I begged her for mercy.

I was startled awake by the face of a cop who was looking at me and trying to determine if I was dead or simply unconscious.

"Holy shit!" I exclaimed as I tried to get away from

him. I was cowering like a monkey who had just been injured and cornered.

"Hey, hey... man, you're okay... I think," he said, trying to remain as calm and authoritative as he could muster. "You look bad, though, buddy... what happened to you? Let's get some clothes on you."

"Holy shit!" exclaimed the piggish-looking cop. "Somebody beat the bejeezus out of you with a weed eater," he said with a piggish grin. "What's that taped to your chest?"

The note taped to my chest had soaked in some of the blood, which was oozing out of the bright red welts apparent on my naked body.

"Consider this your purification, Cliff Lollard. You will not reveal the functioning of the Universe to the masses, which will only bring chaos to the natural order. Should you return to your heretical and disobedient ways, I will return to finish the job at the order of Our Father who art in heaven. 'Withhold not correction from the child: for if thou beatest him with the rod, he shall not die. Thou shalt beat him with the rod, and shalt deliver his soul from Hell. Proverbs 23:13-14.'"

"What the hell does that mean?" the older, fatter

cop asked. "Holy shit, look at your arms!"

The welts on my arms, hands, and covering my entire body were crimson, trailing, pulsing imprints of the letters S,U,S,E,J. I was shocked as I looked in the mirror.

I looked like I had been freshly branded with the name JESUS on every inch of my body. I told the cops what had happened, or what I think had happened. As we looked around we found no evidence that Christina, or in fact anyone, had been in my house but me. After some follow-up questions and snooping around, the cops left. I was tired and hurting, so I took some ibuprofen and went to take a shower.

I was sitting on the couch, trying to take it all in, when the younger officer called me on the phone.

"Mr. Lollard, we have followed up on your information but have run into dead ends all the way around. We went to the cafe where you work, and not one person knew who we were talking about. We went to the address where you say she lived, but what we found was a vacant lot. Are you sure your injuries are not self-inflicted? We just don't have any evidence to go on. You've given us nothing. We'll keep the investigation open, but we've done all we can."

# Wide Awake

Passing through Chimayo, I stop at the diner and I'm reminded of the story that started here. In 1959, it was a dusty, dry little community between Albuquerque and Taos, New Mexico. There was no town so to speak, just this diner, Hank's Garage, a grocery store, and a small building which served as city hall. Big Baby used to come here and have a Coca-Cola on hot summer days. Most of the locals thought he was simple and were afraid of what the Bruja had done to him. The Brujas had once been respected, but by the 1950's they had been pushed to the edges of society. Once considered the elder women, the healers, and advisors for the Indians, they were now pariahs; reduced to folklore, like so much of the Indians' way of life. She had come to raise him when a van full of Beatniks had come through town talking about radical politics and getting the locals all riled up. They had missed the sharp curve headed out of town and tumbled off the side of the mountain. Everyone was killed except for the baby. The law came, made a report, and hauled off the bodies. The infant was left in the care of the town mayor. No-one ever claimed the van, the bodies, or the orphan. Eventually, he got handed to the lowest of society; the Bruja.

To ensure that she would never be alone, she placed a spell on him. By the time he was fifteen, he was 6'3" tall. However, his features had never changed from that of a toddler. His head was disproportionately large for his body and shaped like a bean, his arms were short, his belly round, and his legs never reached their potential. His expression never hardened with the development of his personality. He walked with short, choppy steps. He looked like a giant infant. The locals called him "Big Baby". She had given him an Indian name, but no-one called him Onawa except for Jim.

It was a dry hot summer day when Big Baby and Jim, his only real friend, walked into the diner. Holly had watched them through the front windows. There was not much else to look at; just a few older men with straw hats and black-rimmed glasses talking in hushed tones and sipping coffee. The waitress behind the counter greeted the boys as they walked in.

"Hey Fellas. What'll it be today?"

"Two Coca-Colas, please." Jim slapped a dime down on the counter.

"Why don't you two go talk to that young lady in the corner? She's been waiting on her dad's truck to get fixed all morning. She could use some company."

The boys grabbed their glasses and walked over to where the girl was sitting.

"Hi. Can we sit with you?" Jim was very polite and handsome.

"I'm Holly. What's wrong with your friend?"

"Oh. He's just a little different. A Bruja put a spell on him. He's really very smart."

"Hello Holly. Everyone just calls me Big Baby, for obvious reasons." His smile made him look like a cherub.

"Big Baby, if a witch put a spell on you, there has to be a way to break it. Just look for it. You'll find it, if that's what you want."

"Yes. She won't tell me because she doesn't want me to leave her. She's old and lonely. I care for her because she raised me. I owe her that."

The three of them enjoyed a stimulating conversation. Holly began to feel a connection to the boys. Big Baby was smart and sincere and surprisingly well-adjusted for his predicament. Time seemed to stand still as the day wore on like a dream.

A black Ford kicked up a cloud of dust as it whipped into the parking spot outside the window.

"That's my dad. I guess they got the truck fixed. I'm so sad to go - I've had fun talking to you. My mom died a year ago and my father and I are moving to Arizona to make a new start. I won't know anyone there. If I give you my address, will you write to me?"

"Sure." The boys nodded.

Holly's dad honked the horn and motioned for her to come outside.

"Please write me?" She hugged each of them and thanked them for spending time with her. They watched her get into the truck and head down the highway.

Jim wrote to her in the beginning, but it was Big Baby who was the communicator of the two. He wrote to Holly at least once a month. Jim got the attention of the girls in town and he was soon distracted by other things, while Big Baby and Holly shared their experiences of growing up with letters and an occasional picture. She had dated several boys during high school, but nothing too serious. Big Baby had struggled with his condition and acceptance. There were a few times when he was harassed by kids from another town. The Bruja had gotten older and needed him more often. She taught him the ways of the healer, but she never told him how to break the curse. Jim had graduated from high school and moved to California to find work. Big Baby stayed in Chimayo to take care of the old Bruja. He worked at the diner, cooking and washing dishes. He was too afraid of ridicule to leave town. He felt safe here.

It was 1969, when Big Baby was 25, that he received a letter from Holly saying that they would be passing through town. It had been almost a year since she had last contacted him, so he was happy to hear from her and greatly anticipated her arrival. He became resigned to the facts of his life as he saw them; the Bruja had died, taking with her his chances of reversing the spell. Although he longed to see the larger world, this town and this diner were all he would know.

Holly and her father were listening to the radio as they drove through the desert. Hank Williams was singing "Your Cheating Heart" when the announcer cut in.

"We interrupt our regular programming for this special bulletin. For those of you in the Chimayo region around Pilots Knob and Large Mesa, we've been getting reports of a massive butterfly migration. People are describing the scene as miraculous and amazing. It seems this is a rare species that has rarely been seen in this area, but as of this time literally millions of them are covering the chaparral and the landscape. If you happen to be in the area, be aware that visibility may be low. We now return you to your normal programming." Hank started crooning again.

"That's where we are, but I don't see anything." Holly stated. They drove a mile further when, on the horizon above the heat mirage coming off of the desert, they saw what looked like a dark cloud descending. As they got closer, the cloud seemed to be crawling and alive. They stopped a hundred yards from the edge.

"Holy God in Heaven!" Her father exclaimed.

The entire horizon, from east to west and from the ground to as high as they could see, was a gargantuan living mass of butterflies shading out the sun and covering every object for as far as they could see. They began laughing uncontrollably as the butterflies landed on them and they were soon completely covered. They both laugh and cried with awe and joy to be witnessing this miracle. Just as soon as they appeared, the butterflies drifted off into the distance like a passing rain storm. The two stood there in amazement, covered in a shiny velvety powder; the dust from the wings of the beautiful metallic blue creatures. In a daze, they got back in the truck and continued driving.

They arrived in Chimayo and pulled into the diner parking lot. Not much had changed since they last visited the town ten years ago. Big Baby met them at the door.

Holly spread her arms to hug Big Baby. He squeezed her tight.

"I am so happy to see you!" He said. "What is that blue dust that is all over you?"

"It was so amazing, Big Baby, we saw a miracle in the desert; a giant cloud of butterflies and they landed all over us."

The three of them sat down to lunch and got caught up. Big Baby realized how much Holly had meant to him. She had been a real friend to him, helping him to cope and to accept himself. He was grateful and loved her for it. She had gone to community college in Arizona and was moving out on her own in the near future. He was so happy for her.

"Well, look," she said. "We don't mean to rush off, but we've got business to attend to so we better get going. Let's stay in touch."

Big Baby was sad - he felt this would be the last time he would ever see her. Just like Jim, she was moving on to bigger and better things while he was still in Chimayo. He stood in the parking lot as they drove away. His heart sank in his chest. Maybelle gave him the rest of the day off.

In the middle of the night, Big Baby woke up in a cold sweat. He had a high fever and felt as if a sharp stick had pierced his temple. He thought of dying. He became unconscious. For two days, he lay in a semi-conscious state. Crazy visions of animals and demons flashed through his mind. He felt he had gone insane. On the third day, when the fever broke, he got up and showered. He wasn't feeling himself. He got dressed and walked to town.

When he got to the diner, he could see the old men in the corner staring at him through the window. They pulled their heads closer and whispered. He walked in and said hello to everyone. They all looked at him as if he were a stranger; he had seen that look before.

"What's going on?"

"Can I help you, hun?" asked Maybelle.

"Maybelle, it's me, Big Baby. What's going on?"

She looked confused and did a double take.

"I recognize that voice, but you're not Big Baby. Not the Big Baby I know."

He looked in the mirror behind the bar and broke down into tears. Before him stood a perfectly proportioned body - his vision of himself beneath the spell that had plagued him. That vision had manifested. Something in the butterfly dust had lifted the old Bruja's spell and he was "normal" for the first time in his life. He was crying with joy as he hugged Maybelle, then walked out of the diner. Holly got one letter from him explaining that her miracle in the desert had somehow cured him and that he was free to go and see the world at last.

Every time I come back to this town, I stop in. Nothing has changed. Maybelle still runs the place and people still talk about Big Baby; his absence looms over this place  like a subtle shadow. About a year ago, on my previous visit, I told them that they should all stop calling him Big Baby and start calling him by the name that only his real friends call him: Onawa.

# The Fishing Trip

Two buddies had decided to go on a fishing trip, both men in their late thirties. Oakley had a job at a chemical plant making alcohol derivatives, while Keith worked at another plant loading trucks and rail cars. They had days off together and this was a thing they did, because they were best friends and they both loved fishing. They had gone on fishing tips together since high school. Now and again they took their wives or their children, but this was one of those times when they had both taken some vacation time and were going to spend time on the lake, with the fish.

They were what most people - even their closest friends and family - would consider rednecks. You don't grow up in East Texas without a love for

NASCAR, country music, women, beer, four wheelers, and big pickup trucks. As a man, one also acquires the love for outdoor stuff like hunting and fishing. These guys loved fishing. When they were at work, they talked about fishing. When they were off, they talked about fishing. When they were at home, they watched fishing shows from the comfort of their vibrating recliner chairs. When they slept, they dreamed about fishing. When they weren't thinking about fishing... well, they just weren't thinking at all.

The next day, in the wee hours of the morning, they would make the pilgrimage to one of their favorite fishing places , Fayette Lake near Fayetteville, Texas. This was a man-made lake created for the use of the power plant that sat to the north end of the lake and provided electricity for most of the surrounding area. The water, used for creating steam to turn the giant turbines, was warmed year-round and provided for the exceptional size of the largemouth bass in the lake. On this trip, Keith and Oak were going for the big ones. They would be on the water before dawn, speeding toward their predesignated spot. In the days leading up to this they had packed their rods, their reels, their tackle boxes, and, of course, a cooler full of Bud Light

Beer (standard fishing equipment for around these parts).

Oakley had gone on vacation with his wife to Belize the previous year. While dining at an outdoor café, a local guy had approached them and offered a joint of "some of the best stuff he had ever smoked" in trade for a couple of beers. The trade was made but, fearing a drug test upon returning from a "Caribbean" vacation, Oak did not partake of the herb. Unintentionally and thankfully, the weed went undetected at customs and made it back to the States, stowed away in the pocket of the T-shirt he was wearing that night. She found it while doing laundry and had given it to him. He kept it as a memento of their trip - and for a "special occasion".

Not feeling as concerned at this time about drug testing, and just in case the mood hit them, he decided to bring the joint on this trip. *It's great to commune with nature and catch a little buzz sometimes. It makes the fishing more fun, helps the conversation flow, and just makes things a little more interesting. Besides... I need to let my hair down - or what's left of it - once in a while. I'm a red-blooded American. I should have the*

*Right.* He was feeling a little rebellious, as rednecks often do.

Keith arrived at Oakley's house precisely at 1am. It was a two hour drive from Oak's house; that would put them there at three, boat in the water by three-thirty. Park the truck, give the boat one last quick inspection, load the ice chest, and be sitting at the dock drinking coffee and waiting for the first signs of dawn by 4:25am. In their favorite spot by 5:30am. They had it planned down to the minute, with time to spare and a contingency plan should they need to make an unplanned stop at the store to take a leak or get something that had been missed in the preplanning stage. They were on the road by 1:05am. There was little traffic as they drove through the Houston metro area and another great fishing journey lay ahead of them. It was a moonless night - perfect for fishing at first light. It was late August and there would be no wind, so the water would be as smooth as a mirror. There was an unspoken pride and awareness of the timing and potential of this trip for catching the really big ones. This was going to be a special trip.

They were driving through the night. A glow from the dash instruments cast a greenish hue on the inside of the truck. They were listening to some overnight AM radio show with a guest who was an expert on extraterrestrials from the Pleiades's.

"Do you believe that shit?" piped up Keith after a long silence where each seemed to be lost in higher thought.

"I don't know," Oak replied, "Sounds like they've been smoking the good stuff, or maybe they live to close to a chemical plant or something. Speaking of the good stuff, I brought a doobie that I got in Belize - it's a long story... but I brought it 'just in case'." His facial expression was emotionless as he stared out the windshield at the highway appearing on the edge of the headlights, then passing under the hood of the truck. His eyes were masked by the shadow of his baseball cap.

"What? That's awesome! Wait, aren't you worried about getting piss tested?"

"Not really... it's been a long time since anyone was called up and I've been there forever now, they're not tryin' to bust me. I figure just a little bit at the beginning of my vacation won't show up anyway. It's been forever since I smoked. Besides, I've been saving this for a special occasion; this seems like a special occasion to me. It's like we're heading into the 'Perfect Storm' of fishing."

"What the hell?" Keith asked, rhetorically. "Light it, don't hide it." That was a phrase they used back in high school, when it was a regular thing to be doing. He cracked opened the passenger side window about three inches to suck the smoke out of the truck. The night air was warm and moist as it circulated from the back seat around to where Oakley was still staring out the front windshield. Oak reached into the pocket of his favorite fishing t-shirt and pulled out a pack of Marlboro 100's. The cellophane wrapping made a crisp sound as he handed the pack to Keith.

"It's in here," Oak lifted his hand and lazily pointed as he spoke. He only took his eyes off the road for a second as Keith grabbed the pack from his hand. He looked down at the pack, focused his eyes on Keith's face, grinned, and then squinted back out into the night.

"Fire it up!" he added, as if by habit.

There was a sudden brightness from within the cab of the truck as Keith flicked the lighter and covered the flame and the joint with his left hand. The yellow light of the flame, in contrast with the green of the truck's dash instruments, reflected off the underside of his cap. It was possible to see the central features of his face, his eyes crossed to watch as the flame moved toward the tip. The paper sizzled as the flame touched the tip. Keith drew on the spliff and sucked the flame into the end. There was a small pop and the scent of a grass fire in the distance as the herb began to burn. Keith took the first paper hit and exhaled out the window. Then, he put the joint back to his lips and sucked hard to get that first taste... he held his breath in his chest and choked a little as he passed it to Oak. *Ahh, the passing of the joint. Such a ritually social act. It brings the tribe together on a psychic level.* Keith exhaled a cloud of smoke as Oak raised it to his mouth, pinched between his index finger and his thumb. His middle finger braced against his nose and his ring and pinky finger extended as he savored the extended inhale. He passed it back to Keith. Each took turns, inhaling, holding, choking, passing, exhaling. When the joint was half burnt, Keith raised it to the open passenger window. He squeezed the burning end and rolled it between his fingers until the cherry broke off and sucked out the window. As a matter of old habit, like riding a bicycle, he rolled the window down another couple of inches to "clear the air" inside the cab of the truck. The night air mixed in a delicate bouquet with the acrid smell of the smoke, then faded into humid Texas night air. He rolled the window up.

"That kinda smelled funny," he said after staring out the front windshield for a minute or two.

"Yeah... it's probably old, low-grade stuff." replied Oakley. "Probably won't do much either, but it tasted good and that was fun, like old times, either way." He shrugged his shoulders and squinted back out into the night.

"I'll put this back into your pack," Keith added. "Save the rest for later."

They both stared out the front windshield. Time passed by, marked by the broken white line in the center of the road. Oak noticed that they had started to seem to rush by and he could almost hear them as they passed just left of the driver's side of the truck. Just outside the door. If he rolled down the window, he began to imagine that he could hear the whooshing, rushing, heartbeat of the road as they went by.

"Hey, I think I got a little buzz," he said suddenly.

"Yeah... feels like it's starting to kick in," Keith said. " I think this is creeper weed." He tilted his head a little to the left as he spoke, but he didn't take his eyes off the road. Oakley sensed a subtle drifting of the truck, as if the steering had suddenly become a shade looser under his hands. He lifted his foot some off of the gas pedal. Imperceptibly so; unconsciously.

"Do you know what I think the problem with the world is?" Keith asked, disrupting the hypnosis caused by the sound of the tires on the road.

"No, what?"

"All this political correctness crap."

"What?"

"You know... all this political correctness crap."

"No, tell me."

"Okay... well… you have these people who want to make things fair for everybody, right? When you are a little kid and your mama wants you to play with little Timmy Boodreaux, she tells you to share your toys with him… let's say... you have to let him use your Tonka Dump Truck, so y'all can both play in the sand pile. She'll say... 'be fair', or 'it's only fair to share and let him play with your trucks too'. But then they'll turn around and tell you that if you want a sip of their beer... 'No, it's not for kids'. But 'it's not fair' you cry. What is their response? What is the first thing they say to you?

"I don't know. What?"

"Life is not fair, little Oakley. Whoever told you life was fair?"

"Dude," Oakley laughed, "You're stoned. What does what you just said have anything to do with political correctness? You should leave the heavy thinking to educated liberal academics. Just stick with fishin'. That's about as deep as you need to go." They both laughed uncontrollably for a time. A good deep belly laugh.

"The mind is a terrible thing..." Oakley added. This initiated another round of uncontrollable laughter. "Ohhh shit! That's funny," he said, wiping a tear from the corner of his eye.

The laughter slowly subsided and they both stared out the windshield into the night.

"What time is it?", Keith asked. He looked at his watch and the clock on the dash. "Two AM, right on time. Man... we're half way there already."

"We'll be there in no time. Do you want to stop at the next truck stop? We can get some coffee. Nothing goes better with weed than coffee. Besides, I need to take a leak."

"Sure. We have plenty of time," answered Keith. The rolling of the road and the night out the windshield slowly grabbing their attention again.

On the horizon appeared the faint and familiar sign of the truck stop. Like a beacon in the night high above the ground, really high, a hundred feet or more. It was the most prominent thing in the field of view for miles around. A gathering place, relative safety, an oasis in the featureless, dark desert of the night. They both shifted in their seats, an unconscious reaction to the pressure their bladders created, relieved to be so close to a restroom. As they got closer, Oakley exited off the highway and onto the access road. There was a stop sign and a sharp right turn, then an almost immediate left across a Farm to Market road. As they pulled in, the boat trailer, which they were pulling behind the truck, caught the curb with the left side wheel. The trailer hopped up and down, making a jerking motion in the cab of the truck.

"Holy shit! I forgot that was back there", Oak replied. Uncontrollable laughter erupted in the dark, green-lit cab of the truck. Laughing until tears rolled down their cheeks, they pulled up to the gas pump, stopped the truck, and got out. The truck stop was clean and well-lit. Oak and Keith felt self-conscious as they walked in, they were both kinda stoned.

When you're stoned and have been in nature or isolated away from people, it is always a shock and a litmus test of how stoned you are when you first encounter people or society. Suddenly, you must interact with non-stoned reality and it is a bit like being pushed out onto a stage in front of a crowd without any planned script or act. Society has rules and boundaries and expectations and stands in stark contrast to stoned reality which is fluid, less rigid, and has fewer expectations. It is you, up there, with the intensity of the spotlight and the pressure of all eyes focused on you. So, it takes you a minute or so to acclimate and figure out a plan of action or behavior.... and try not to appear too stoned, because everybody knows you're stoned. Or so you think.

The bathrooms were clean. However, there's always that pair of shoes under the door of the stall at the far end of the room. Shoes with a pair of pants bunched up around them. The odor is subtle at first and you really have to get a few whiffs to appreciate it fully. *Yep... that's shit. Wow! What did that guy eat? You can tell a lot about a person by the smell of their shit, most of it unconsciously.* Then there's the little farting sound, a little too wet and forceful. It was all they could do to not laugh out loud when the man, assuming it was a man, as it was the men's room after all, let out a grunt like a pig rooting contentedly in the woods, just as the splash of a turd hitting the water could be heard.

"Let's get out of here," Keith managed, barely able to contain himself as he wiped his hands with a paper towel and threw it in the silver rimmed-hole in the center of the wash counter. The quality of sound! Their voices and their shoes hitting the floor was crisp, echoed, and affected by the pungent humidity of the bathroom. They were giggling as they entered the store proper and perused the isles. Truck stops were always an odd mixture of travel necessities. Some things you may need in an emergency, like a tire patching kit or a pair of gloves. They also have a lot of impulse buy stuff, like an airbrushed painting of Elvis laminated onto a stained piece of wood and finished with a glossy shellack. I guess people must have bought those in the past, as they are ubiquitous. Always present, always watching, always for sale. There always seems to be an abundance of cellphone accessories. Truckers love cellphone accessories, something you may not have known. They both grabbed a cup of coffee and stood in line to pay for it. People are interesting in the middle of the night. The counter help tend to be extremely obese women who smell strange and look unhappy. They're a bit like shift workers, they have the same tired look in their eyes. The customers are an odd mixture of travelers trying to get somewhere and partiers trying to either get to the next party or home. There's always that one guy who you suspect might be carrying a body in the trunk of his car or looking for one to put there. They paid for their coffee and returned to the truck.

"I didn't realize how stoned I was until I walked into that store," Keith stated.

"Yeah, then it felt like everyone was staring at us. I hate being stoned in public."

Oakley got back in on the driver's side, slammed the door shut, started his truck, and pulled out. There was a loud crunching noise as he made the immediate left out of the fuel pump area.

"Oh shit," Oakley chuckled, "I forgot that was back there." Their boat trailer had destroyed a trash can as it pulled up over the end of the pump island. They both laughed until they thought they would piss on themselves.

"You better be careful. We don't wanna get stopped by the cops. Not now!" They pulled out of the parking lot and onto the access road. They built up speed as they merged onto the highway and into the night. Twenty minutes or so passed. The terrain was changing from coastal flood plain to rolling hills. Looking out the window as they crested some of the higher hills, the number of stars in the sky was amazing. Neither Keith nor Oak could ever remember seeing so many stars. They pondered their cosmic insignificance, each in their own way, as they stared out the windows. On the hilltop a few miles away, they could see headlights. At night here, houses on the side of the road seemed to be the only thing moving as they sped past the windows and quickly faded back into the night.

"Sometimes, man," Oak paused, lost in thought, "I don't know really how to say it, using big words, but... I feel like I'm on an atom or something.... like we are atoms, from a rock or something, and those stars and the planets, which seem so far away from us, if we were looking at that rock held in our hand, were just other atoms inside the rock, if you could just get closer and closer to that rock, and smaller and smaller. Did that make sense? You know what I'm trying to say?"

"Nope," Keith answered. He never took his eyes from the night sky, searching, searching for understanding.

"Are you listening to me, Keith? I'm having an 'Apifany' thing here and you are over there about to drool on yourself. You know, Einstein or somebody like that said, 'The universe is mostly made of empty space'."

"Yeah. I'm listenin'. Oak, how long have we known each other?" Then, answering his own question with a question, "Most of our lives. Right?"

"Yeah, that's right. Why?"

"You know God didn't make the universe out of 'empty space'. The earth is solid. Buddy, it's solid. A rock ain't got no empty space in it. I don't even try to think about stuff like that. It's too complicated, besides preacher says that information is only out there to confuse and tempt us. So why are you askin; these questions?"

"Think about it, Keith, don't be a bump on a log. What is God?"

"Slow down, Oak..."

"No! I won't. Why can't we ask these questions. Didn't God give us a brain to use?"

"No..! SLOW DOWN!"

"I'm a grown man - don't raise your voice to me."

Keith points out the window, speechless, frantic.

"OOOOH SHHHHIIIIIITT!"

Headlights flashed into the cab of the truck, a camera shot of their terror-stricken faces as they both slammed their feet to the floor board to apply the brakes and brace themselves for a head on impact. Out of pure reflex, Oakley yanked the wheel to the right. The truck and boat made a quick serpentine evasive maneuver. A dip net catapulted out of the boat and made a rasping sound as it slid beneath the oncoming pickup and into the tall grasses on the other side of the highway. A tackle box rolled and bounced as it hit the warm aggregate. Tires squealed. The other truck dipped to the shoulder, close call. Very close. Oakley wrestled the truck to a stop, half-on and half-off the shoulder of the road. He sat there, two hand death grip on the wheel, heaving his breath. He looked over at Keith.

"You okay?" he asked, his voice trembling like he might cry.

Silence.

"You okay?" he asked again, stronger, more emotional.

Keith took a deep breath in, his first, and nodded his head. His ball cap was loose and high on the crown of his head.

"Oh my God," Oakley breathed out, taking his right hand from the wheel and placing it on his chest. "That was close."

He suddenly caught some snap and looked out the rear view mirror, just as the other truck's tail lights topped a hill a few miles behind them and disappeared into the black.

"They didn't even stop," he whispered, puzzled. "Guess they're OK."

"Good graciousness," said Keith, shaking off the shock, "we almost just died."

They both looked at each other in the eye for what was, in reality, just a few seconds, but for them it was as if in slow motion, an effect of the adrenalin. Suddenly, they both erupted into nervous laughter. Uncontrollable, gut-squeezing laughter. They laughed until they were out of breath. Suddenly, a black and white Highway Patrol car topped the hill and flashed past them at a high rate of speed. They both sat up straight and froze. At night in these hills, you could hear a vehicle coming for miles. At first it is a low purr, like a faint train horn in the distance. As the car passed they could hear the pitch crescendo, then at predictable intervals descend, back to a faint purr, and fade out. They both turned their heads to see the tail lights disappear over the next hill. Then, the realization came that the reason the other truck did not stop was the same reason that the patrol car did not stop.

"Hot pursuit."

They both laughed again for a solid five minutes.

"Let's go check everything out, I think I heard something hit the highway when we got out of the way. I can't believe that guy was driving so fast, and on the wrong side of the road."

As Oakley stepped out of the truck, he realized that he was on a two lane highway divided by a yellow line. It had actually been him who was on the wrong side of the road and it had been that way since he exited off of the interstate; at least 12 miles in hills. He shook his head at the thought of what could have just happened. He wasn't laughing.

"Hmmph," he just shook his head.

They walked around until they found the net and the tackle box. The road always seems wider when you're standing on it. From a vehicle, you cannot perceive this fact. The road seems narrower from behind the dash, nor can you appreciate what a hill top, at night, in this part of the country is like. The night breeze was cool and there were lights off in the distance, no doubt, from houses. A pack of coyotes sang into the night like wild banshees. A chill ran up Keith's spine as he gazed up at the sky.

"Man, it is beautiful out here," he exclaimed. "Look at that and tell me there ain't no God."

"Sure is beautiful." Oakley agreed.

They stood there for an undetermined amount of time. There was not much traffic on the road at this time of the night, out here.

"Hey look!" Keith finally said. "There's the power plant."

Sure enough, to the north of where they were standing, two flashing lines of white lights rose into the sky. From this distance you could not see the stacks of the coal burning power plant, but the flashing column lights were a familiar sight around these parts. Like a lighthouse, or a beacon, it was a point of reference. Just above the tree line you could see a faint halo of light, as if a shining pot of silver sat at the end of the strobing rainbow of the night.

"There it is," said Oak, staring longingly and in awe. "We're close."

"Yep."

They stood there for some time. Silent. Reverent. It was a beautiful sight.

"Hey, let's get back on the road... it's got to be getting late, or early. We're gonna get off schedule," Oak finally said.

"Yeah, let's go."

They got back in the truck. It was 2:30 in the morning. At this point, all I can say is that they arrived at the boat ramp at 4:45am. Any and everything that happened in the next two hours and 15 minutes was a complete blur, including the reason it took them that long to travel 15 miles and how they had planned for two extra hours in their trip, either accidentally or by coincidence. In their minds, all that remained were the road, the night sky, and the oaks. The stacks of the plant and the facility grew larger and larger as they approached. The ambient light grew more and more, as if the dawn of a moon three times the size of Earth's colored the sky the deepest of blues and bathed the environment around them. The contrast of this feat of modern engineering stood out against the night, a monolith of what man can accomplish with the intellect and the resources. The light against the live oaks created a dream-type light of silver and shadows.

"Dammit. We're 20 minutes late," Keith broke the silence.

"Yeah, well, I'm in no hurry now bud."

"Yeah, well… we better get movin' if we're gonna be there by dawn."

"Look, Keith, buddy, let's take some time to appreciate where we are, man."

"I'll appreciate getting my line wet. That's what we are here for."

"Keith, you need to learn to relax. Breathe."

"You always get like this. I knew this would happen."

"What?"

"You, man, you always get this way when you're stoned."

"No, I don't. YOU always get like THIS."

"Like what?"

"Keith, buddy, forget it. It's nothin'. Let's go fishin'. That's what we're here for, right?"

"Right. Let's go."

Oakley backed the boat down the ramp and into the water, with Keith's expert hand signals and a sense of team work developed through many such entries. Everything went off without a hitch. The boat was launched and tied to the wooden plank dock. The water was dark and alive. The light from the power plant refracted off the ripples of the slick-moving surface and reflected back up at the stars as if the two were in a quiet dialogue in a secret, symbolic language. There were no other boats, trucks, or humans at the ramp. They had it all to themselves. Oakley parked the truck not too far from the boat ramp, got out, locked it, and made one last check around before heading down to the boat.

"I think we got everything," he said. "Let's get the show on the road."

He stepped off the dock and into the boat. Keith had already done final checks on fuel, batteries, and gear. He was behind the wheel and ready to start the engine.

"Hey, wait a minute. Let's light this thing up again before we get movin'," said Oakley as he pulled the cigarette pack out of his pocket. "We can't start this epic fishing adventure without first getting our heads on straight."

"I don't know man. I'm still stoned. Aren't you?"

"Yeah, but I want to be REALLY stoned," replied Oak.

Keith lifted his hand in the air and waved it lackadaisically, grinned, and shook his head in submission and agreement.

"Light it, don't hide it," he resigned.

The engine turned over with a short growl as the smell of gasoline and exhaust wafted past. They slowly idled out of the ramp area and toward open water. The lights of the console made their faces stand out against the darkness as they glided along slowly. The lake stretched out before them, awesome in its expanse, and seemed to stretch out beyond the horizon into the black night. They passed the remainder of the joint until it was too small to hold. Keith, taking the last hit, flicked it over the edge and into the lake as if making a small offering to the gods of fishing. He held the smoke in his chest as he looked, once more, at the GPS and the depth finder. He looked at Oak and nodded, then blew out smoke in synch with his hand moving forward on the throttle. The boat pulled out of the water and planed on top of the surface. The propeller churned the water behind them, making a triangle of white foam as they sped off into the night.

"Are you okay going this fast at night on the lake?" Oakley asked, shouting over the muffled whine of the engine.

"Yeah man, I know this lake like the back of my hand. Besides, I'm used to your instruments and we're out here in the deep channel. We're good. We've got GPS and we can practically see under water with this bad ass fish finder you've invested in.";

"That's true. I do appreciate the finer things in fishing."

They looked at each other and started laughing. They each knew that good gear was essential to effective fishing, but sometimes they went a little overboard, no pun intended, to get the latest and greatest thing, often to the griping and nagging of their wives who had more domestic priorities, like groceries.

"Hey, how about a cold one?" Keith asked with enthusiasm.

"Does a bear shit in the woods?" asked Oak as he reached back over into the cooler and grabbed two cans. He opened his with a snap and took a big swig. "Damn, it don't get any better than this."

"Nope."

"Hey, did you think it was strange that nobody else was at the boat ramp?" asked Keith

"Now that you think of it, that is kinda strange."

"Why isn't anyone else fishing?"

"That's a good question. I don't see anyone else out moving either. We're almost to the center of the lake. Let's shut the boat down for a second and see if we can hear any other boat motors moving across the lake."

Keith slowed the boat to a putter, then turned the key off. They sat there, each looking to the horizon for any lights and scanning the night with their hearing for signs of another boat. Nothing. Just the hum of the power plant and the sounds of the night. Even from the center of the lake, the towers seemed to reach into the heavens, the power plant was of mountainous size. They sat and stared at it for some time, the boat gently rocking with the motion of the water.

At the same instance, they both seemed to notice that everything in their world seemed to shift to the left about three inches. It was disorienting and they both sat there in the boat in the dark, trying to adjust their senses to the sharp movement.

"Did you see that?"

"I saw something," Oak said, shaking his head.

"I think I'm fucked up man."

"Yeah, me too. Really fucked up."

"What was in that shit, man? I ain't thinking right."

"I don't know. It came all the way from Belize. Dude said it was the best."

"I think there was something else in that because this ain't like nothin' I felt before. Are we gonna be OK?"

"I don't know, Keith. I don't know."

"Well hey, let start up the boat and... go somewhere."

"Where Keith? Where are we gonna go?"

"I don't know... can you get us back to the boat ramp?"

Keith was beginning to have a hard time gathering his thoughts; they seemed to be scattered about the boat and bobbing up and down in the water. He was unable to focus on the GPS and it intimidated him to begin changing the displays. He looked out at the reflections on the water. It seemed as if the night sky extended into the water below him. He got a chill, a sense of vertigo, and grabbed the side of the boat to steady himself.

"Wow! It is a beautiful night," he stood now, confidently looking up at the sky with outstretched arms. A tear formed in the corner of his right eye. It was simply too much beauty. It had been there all along and he had never noticed it before. A child's sense of wonder passed through his consciousness, out his feet, and into the universe. The ripples in the water made arcs as they flowed out of the lake, through the boat, and off into the heavens.

"It is so beautiful." He began to weep. "It's so beautiful."

"Dude? Dude? Are you okay?" asked Oak concerned. "Dude, I'm fighting it too. This sucks. I'm starting to have a bad trip." There was shakiness of emotion rising in his voice.

"The universe is in perfect balance now. If we choose, we may simply slip into this higher frequency and we can see, at once, our full potential."

"Man, can you get us back to the truck?" Oak asked.

"Yes I can, my friend. I don't want this to sound wrong, but... I love you, man. I really love you. I will get us back... I got a handle on this."

Keith fired up the boat and, with a sputter and a growl, he thrust the gears and the throttle forward. The boat lifted out of the water and slid through the universe, reflected in the lake. It was if they were skating on smooth ice as they sliced through the night. Oakley stood to the right of the console. He stared out into the night, looking for obstructions in the water despite the fact that he was verbally unable to express what he was doing. They traveled in this manner for a solid 20 minutes, both silent, both looking out into the night. Keith had a look of wonderment on his face as he held the wheel and gazed out into the night.

Suddenly, Oakley started waving his hands. He held down his ball cap with his left and pointed with his right arm at something off the right bow. He turned to Keith, held his mouth open, and pointed and snapped his fingers as if this would help him to conjure the words. He looked out into the water and did it again. Frantically, he jumped into the water and hit it with a slap and a roll as Keith sped off looking back at where his friend had just gone overboard. He cut the throttle and circled back to his left.

"Oh my God! Oh my God!" he repeated to himself as he approached where he thought he had last seen his friend. "Oh my God, oh my God!"

He slowly crept past the area where he thought Oak might be. He noticed that there were a few trees in the area, this was not a good sign. Oak could be trapped under a log, or stuck in the mud at the bottom of the lake. He could be anywhere. He circled back to the left for another pass when some movement in the water caught his eye off the starboard bow. It was Oak and he was frantically swimming off toward the direction of a clump of trees, like he was trying to get away from a gator or something. Keith caught up with him and pulled alongside.

"Hey! What the hell are you doing man? You scared the shit out of me!" Keith hollered.

Oakley stopped swimming and looked up at his friend.

"I'm sorry," he said, out of breath. "Did you see that?"

"See what?"

"Her," he pointed back over his shoulder.

"No. Dude, we're in the middle of the lake. What 'her' are you talking about?"

"Her. There was a woman, kinda, swimming off to the side of the boat. I swear to God."

"What do you mean 'kinda'?" Keith asked.

"She was swimming over here," he pointed in the same direction.

"Who?" Keith insisted.

"The sexy Sasquatch woman." There was an awkward silence following his statement. "She was swimming off in this direction, as god is my witness." He raised his hand out of the water as if swearing on a Bible. "We've got to follow her."

"Dude, you could have killed yourself! You've got a wife and kids, you can't be doing crazy shit like that."

"Keith, we're gonna follow her. Don't try to change the subject," Oakley said as he began a fit of uncontrolled laughter.

"Why are we going to follow her? You know this is crazy right?"

"Because, just because. It's the right thing to do. Help me in," Oak was serious.

He extended his hand and Keith helped him into the boat. "Dude, we have to catch her. Get going!" he said. Water was dripping off of him and beading up on the floor of the boat. Pointing again off the right bow of the boat, he motioned for Keith to get moving.

"Okay, okay." Keith often unconsciously did what Oak told him to do. It had been that way since they were kids. In Keith's mind a scene plays out: early in the past, two young boys are playing in a sand pile - one a strawberry-blond and chubby cheeked boy with freckles and missing some front teeth, the other brown-haired, thinner, and quiet in "Big Mac" bib coveralls and a Gilligan hat. A big green grasshopper comes clicking down between them, it's eyes two black orbs. The freckle-faced boy slams a hand down on top of it, lifts it between his index finger and thumb, grabs the head with the same fingers on the other hand, and unceremoniously separates the head from the body.

"Here, you pull the legs off," he says with a callous grin. He pokes the grasshopper at the other. The other stares.

"Okay," he reaches for the bug.

"You stop that right now!" says an intelligent forty-ish woman in a key lime polyester dress and cat eye glasses. She points her finger at the brown-haired boy.

"You know what your heart is saying to you, don't you? You know what you're about to do ain't right!"

"Yes, ma'am!" Keith responds obediently.

"And you," she pauses and points to the freckle-faced boy, "you, you know better too. Don't be showing him things like that. If you do something like that again, I'm gonna take a hickory switch to you, do you understand?"

"Yes ma'am," he started to cry and dig a hole in the sand beside a giant yellow Tonka truck.

Oakley had a vision of the same story from the opposite perspective, but he had forgotten how sad he felt when he thought "Ain't Effie" was gonna take a switching to him. And a hickory switch at that. He always liked her and knew he was going down a wrong path; it was a leap forward in his development. It was a small miracle. He was never cruel to an animal again. Even in fishing he always treated the fish in a way that he felt any living being deserved. He even said a silent "thank you" to every fish he ever caught, but he didn't remember crying so much.

# Chapter 2

The Sasquatch woman story really began when Oakley was about eleven, precisely the time when he was at an impressionable point in his sexual development, and he saw an episode of "In Search Of.." with Leonard Nimoy while on a fishing trip with his parents. It had been this peculiar, secret desire all along, in his heart-of-hearts, to fall passionately in love with a woman of the forest. It was just how an 11 year old boy's mind works sometimes in regard to early sexual fantasies. It was so bizarre to him that he had even had the thought, that he didn't even realize that it was his deepest desire. It was totally and unconsciously pushed away by a sense of morals and codes, labeling it as abhorrent - but *this* time, *this* was not a fantasy. She was actually here, swimming off to their northwest and getting further away.

"Hey, let's not just sit here. Go!" Oakley punched Keith in the shoulder.

"Hey," Keith rubbed his shoulder. He grabbed the wheel, pushed the throttle up a bit, and off they sped.

Chasing the Sasquatch woman. They pulled up into a flat cove with a mass of cattails and broad grasses.

"Slow down, slow down," Oakley directed. "Over there, over there." Again to the right of the boat there was a parting in the reeds. "This way, this way, look. Look."

"I don't see anything," Keith stated. Reeds opened up to a smaller cove, a lagoon, that met up with the shore. A fog was forming in the predawn coolness. He shivered against the cool moisture on his face and hands. The eastern sky was turning violet. He paused and looked at the sky. The water reflected the sky under a high patch of fog and he had the realization that these were the perfect conditions for bass to feed. Big bass. There was a moment of silence and an experience of the larger sense of nature.

"Hey. Dude."

"Yeah, Keith?"

"This is it."

"What?"

"This is what we came here for."

"What?"

"This moment, right now. Dude, look at the sky. Look at the water. This fog, this cove. Dude, it is time to fish. Now," Keith grabbed Oak's shoulders and nodded his head as he spoke.

"You're right."

They grabbed their fishing poles and cast out into the glassy black water. Something hit Keith's bait on the first cast - something big!

"Ohh my Goddd," Oakley whispered excitedly. He reeled in as fast as he could.

A sense of deep calm enveloped their sphere of awareness - a sense that only one can get when nature is presenting itself in a way that speaks directly, in a language that only the deepest senses can understand or feel.

Keith reeled his line in with zen-like oneness; he was one with the bait. The water swirled somewhere off to their left and a subtle wave pressed against the top of the water as it passed under the boat.

WHOOM!

Something hit Oakley's line like a mule kicking the side of a barn, or a shotgun blast. He set the hook gently and pulled to keep the feel in the line, not muscle the fish toward the boat. The fish made a run and stripped out the reel as the drag squealed. Oakley lifted the end of his rod. The beast leapt from the water and flapped it's body like it was trying to fly, making a deep percussion in the water when it came back down.

"Did you see that?" Keith asked with graveness in his voice.

"Get the net."

"Yes... Get the net." Keith turned to grab the net.

Suddenly, the line went slack. Oakley lifted the end of the rod and reeled in fast to take the slack out of the line. Nothing.

"What happened?" he complained. "What? Where's my fish?" He reeled his line in. The line had snapped or cut on something in the water.

They stood there, Oakley with a rod in one hand and the end of the line in the other, Keith with his arms down at his sides. Both men were silent. The looked out into the water around them as if a shark were circling their boat, each asking the same question in their mind: "Where is it?" There was a profound stillness. Suddenly, a fish head the size of a Labrador retriever's pops out of the water beside the boat."

"Hey, how was that fight? Did it feel like you really had me?" the words came out, but the mouth and the jaw never moved and the fish's mouth stayed wide open. Both men yelled out loud, terrified of what they were seeing.

"Hey... Hey!... HEY!" the fish got louder and more authoritative. The men caught their snap and stared at the fish. "You can have this back." The fish flung the propylene worm onto the side of the boat, along with about a foot of translucent mono-filament line. "You guys, don't be such *women* about this."

"What do you mean, *women?*" Keith asked defiantly.

"All this 'Aaaahh' and 'Booohooing'. Come on guys. I'm just a fish, probably the best-looking fish you ever saw, but I'm just one of the guys. Get a hold of yourselves."

"But… You're a fish. How can you talk?" asked Oakley

"That's complicated, much too complicated for you, 'Oakley', so I'll spare you the details."

Oakley squinted his eyes a little and looked past the fish, into the water. He was chewing on what the fish had said.

"Look, don't be hurt. It's just complicated. Okay?" the fish said, showing his first hint of compassion. "Just be aware that I am a fish and I'm talking to you. That's all you need to know."

"Okay."

"Look… I love this sport just as much as you. I didn't get to be this big, or this 'handsome', by being easy to catch. Get it? I've been perfecting my game for years. It's my thing. It's what I do. Don't be so surprised you fell for it , there's a reason bass are considered a game fish."

"I'm not sure I know what you mean, Mr. Fish," Keith stated.

"Why am I not surprised?" he rolled his eyes to indicate his annoyance.

Keith looked at Oak and then back at the fish.

"I don't even know how to respond to that."

"Respond to what?"

"Exactly Keith, exactly," he shook his head from side to side, making small rings of disappointment in the water. "Hey, look, I'd really love to stay and chat with you idiots, but I've got shit to do. Okay? Besides, remember the Sasquatch lady? *Well*, she's getting away."

"Yeah…" the guys both looked at each other then back to the fish.

"This will be your only chance, Oakley. This is a once in a life time thing, you can't make this stuff up, but you should go alone from here." He pointed over his left shoulder, with a fin that suddenly resembled a hand, onto the shore and toward a grove of live oaks. "I'll stay here with Keith and make sure he doesn't get into any trouble. All right? Go!" The fish motioned again with his fin and his body.

"Well... Okay. This is really weird, but... Dude..." he looked at his lifelong friend "I gotta go on this one. I don't think I can go on if I don't see this through to the end."

"What are you talking about, Oak?"

"I can't explain... it's complicated."

Keith looked sad, but proud. He knew this was a turning point in their lives. Oak would never be the same again. He had to boldly dive into the unknown and, despite his fears of his own destruction, he would be born into a new life no matter what path he chose at this point. One path leaning forward into life, or the other fleeing from it. It was his rite of passage; his prime directive; the crossroads. He looked at his friend, he looked at the fish, he took a deep breath, and he nodded.

"I can't go back."

"No, you can't," said the fish

Oakley smiled rapturously. He lifted his arms to the heavens and looked out into the predawn sky. He breathed deeply and consciously. A tear formed in the corner of his eye before he gracefully dove into the water. There was a moment of tension as Keith and the fish watched for him to surface. Oak suddenly shot up through the surface, his head covered with mud and spitting the silt out of his mouth. The water he was standing in was only waist deep, abdomen deep if you count the fact that he was standing in six inches of loose, silty bottom strata. The fish laughed loudly, almost maniacally, like some crazy uncle. So did Keith. Oakley turned and trudged off into the night in the direction of the forest woman.

He came to a spot where the mud was drier. He stood there, dripping, out of breath, and using all of his senses to determine which way the Bigfoot girl went. He didn't really know what to expect and got momentarily distracted by the thought of what he was really doing. This seemed so crazy and so right at the same time. This had to be some kind of sign, but how would he explain to his family, his wife? What if he got killed by this animal? Wow? What if...? He brought himself back to the present. He couldn't think about the consequences. Not now. "She went *this* way," he pointed and followed his own direction. He was drawn forward by a scent. Yes, that was it, he could smell her - a wave traveled down his body at his realization of his attraction to her smell. It was subtle and earthy, giving him an experience of bliss he had never encountered before. It was like being in love. He followed a small path through some brush which opened out into a circular group of giant, sprawling, live oaks. There was an opening to the sky in the middle where their canopies did not meet. The sky was beginning to turn red and the shadows beneath the trees were their deepest. His attention was drawn to his 3'o'clock right. He froze. What had called his attention? Was it movement? He struggled to slow his breathing as his heart began to beat out of his chest. A breeze passed his cheek and he caught a whiff of a different smell, but it had the same effect on him; intoxicating. He slowly looked to his right and, on the tree behind him, he saw a pair of soft, yellow eyes. They were feminine eyes.

"I've been waiting for you," came a sultry voice from the direction of the eyes.

Oakley squinted to gather more light with his eyes. What he could make out in the shadows before him was a large woman - at least 6' 4", at least 250 lbs, with a very athletic body totally covered in course hair. It was as you would expect a Sasquatch's hair to be, but hers looked manicured, combed, and she was wearing a fitted tropical dress that totally matched the colors of the lightening morning sky. Her face was attractive, neither apish nor human. In fact, her attractiveness could not be totally calibrated into human proportions, but she was mesmerizing. Her eyes were wild and carried a wisdom that seemed to stare right into the center of his heart.

"Who are you?"

"You don't remember, but once when you were a young boy, your father and mother brought you fishing here. It looked a lot different then. You came to this grove of trees and fished just off this bank. I, too, was a young doe and I stood at the edge of this grove and watched you for hours. I felt a connection to you, but I didn't know why. Your parents called you to leave. You cast your line one more time and caught a small bass. He was just a yearling. You looked at him with a grateful heart and told him thank you for the experience. You set him free. I could feel in your heart that you truly respected life and the life of the forest and *this* place. My heart became one with yours and, as you left, I set an intention to have you come back to me on the day that I am ready to go into heat. I have waited because I had much life to live, but now I want to 'settle down' - to have a baby. I want you to be my mate.

"What...? I don't really understand."

"We don't have much time. The sun is coming up and then my cycle will be finished. I want you to be my mate. I want you to father my baby."

"Okay! Okay! I'll do it," he felt so turned on by her smell, her size, and her fertility power, it was overwhelming. He felt deep within his male spirit the receptivity of her genes. He was driven by primal urge. He pulled his pants down. He was almost painfully erect and swollen, bigger than it had ever been before. He climbed up onto the tree where she was laying and she pulled up her dress to reveal an amazing vagina. It was a work or art. So beautiful, like a soft flower, and much larger than a human's. Oakley felt amazingly turned on. He grabbed around her waist beneath her breasts and entered her. He looked deeply into her eyes. She smelled of the most amazing natural scent you can imagine, like a fine smoked meat. He buried his face in her fur. It was rougher than he imagined. As he fully entered her, he was overwhelmed and reached his climax almost instantly. The spasm of his ecstasy drove his hips in a sewing machine-like fashion. He had feelings of warmth and slime. It was bliss.

"Are you kidding me?" she said. "I've waited all these years for *this?* You have got to be kidding me."

"Huh?" Oak was passing out, his energy spent. Done. He fell asleep on the Sasquatch woman's stomach. He started to drool.

The sun was up when Keith finally found him. He was asleep, laying on an oak tree, his pants around his ankles. Keith shook him awake. Oak came to and backed down out of the tree. He had morning wood and it was stuck inside a knot hole in the trunk of the tree. His penis was chafed and bruised. He looked down at his sore little "friend".

"Where'd the Sasquatch woman go?" he asked, surprised. "Where'd she go?"

"Dude. Dude. She's gone. Okay, she gone. Calm down," Keith grabbed him by the shoulders and shook him a little and looked into his eyes. "Don't tell me you were doing it with a tree."

"No. No, it was her. She wanted me to mate with her. I swear."

"Oh my God," Keith wanted to laugh. It was painful for him to hold it back.

"Don't laugh."

"Okay, okay. Pull yourself together."

Oakley buttoned up his pants and tucked in his shirt.

"I need to find my wallet and my phone," he patted his pockets and looked around.

"We need to get back," Keith said.

"Where are we?"

"I don't really know. The water is back over there," he pointed. "About a thirty-minute walk. What the hell happened back here?"

"I'll tell you on the way back. I found my stuff, let's get out of here."

Neither of them said a word as they made the trek back to the boat, both lost in thought, feeling dull, and still a little messed up. What a night. When they got back to the boat, they found their stuff just as they left it, one line still in the water, the other laying on the deck with the broken line and the lure.

"What about the fish?" asked Oakley.

"What about it.?" Keith shrugged his shoulders and gave Oak a look that he didn't quite understand.

"Well, that's a pretty ambiguous statement. Don't ya think?"

"Don't use big words, it makes you sound smart."

They both laughed until their sides hurt.

"Let's go. I don't know what happened up here and I don't really want to," said Keith. He stared at his life-long friend.

Keith climbed into the boat and started the engine. Oakley pushed it off of the mud and hopped onto the bow, hitching down the line as they backed out of the cove. As they neared the outlet to the bigger cove, Oakley looked back. Standing on the shore he thought he could make out the Bigfoot Girl in her dress, standing on the bank by the trees. He shook his head and shivered. He turned out toward the lake. The outboard revved up and the boat lifted out of the water; it shot out across the lake in the direction of the boat ramp. Neither man said a word.

# Lipstick, Fedora

A friend of mine was throwing a party at her house. The house was moderate and minimalistic in its decor. Its design was reminiscent of the art deco era; everyone attending was ultra-modern metro cool. This was not a crowd to get overly rowdy or loud, mostly understated intellectual types. There were several conversations happening in the room and everyone was either having a cocktail or a glass of wine. There was a bar in the house and someone, I don't know if they were hired or a volunteer, was tending. Most conversations were about art, politics, or the music scene and how commercial, or trendy, it had become and centered around one or two people who were either the expert or most respected veteran of the scene that night.

I had come to the party as a guest of the homeowner. She and I had worked together on a few projects in the past and we seemed to hit it off pretty well when we were together. I had considered dating her and maybe she felt the same way, I didn't really know. Either way, she had called to invite me and here I was. It was a typical party, very quiet this early in the evening and before the drink had really taken effect. Before people's tongues, as well as their attitudes, were well-lubricated. I was making my rounds, seeing whom was present that I might know.

The center of the conversation in the spacious open living room was a tall, dark haired fellow with a rather large angular nose and thin lips. He had brown eyes and a serious look on his face. He was talking about quantum physics and how the possibility of inter-dimensional travel is "theoretically possible". He wore a dark gray jacket over a black turtle neck shirt. He wore black slacks, black dress shoes, and black socks. He was using his hands to express himself. The way he clasped and unclasped his hands gave the impression that he was holding an invisible slinky. His fingers were long and boney and the skin on his hands and face was thin and pallid. He stood against the back drop of the limestone fireplace. In his circle of influence and attention were maybe seven or eight people who listened attentively; some simply looking, others periodically nodded in agreement.

Occasionally, someone would ask a question or contend with a point, often just to show that they could keep the ball in the court if not to make a salient point. Then, perhaps, they would nod as if to say "touche" and look around for approval from the others. Then, their attention would be slowly drawn back to the man in the gray suit. Thereby, the discussion continued. I have to say that he *was* charismatic and it seemed like he knew what he was talking about. It was a bit heavy of a conversation for me, so I stood and watched for a good five minutes before I quietly excused myself and went to see who else may be making an appearance.

I turned to the right and walked into the kitchen area. It was a nicely decorated kitchen, with an avocado toaster and chrome tube chairs with pink marbled vinyl seats and backs, matching the plastic linoleum table top. A simple vase and flowers stood out in contrast to the sterility of the furniture. It was a groovy kitchen.

There was a heavy-set redheaded woman in a denim jacket who was telling the story of something that had happened at work. I caught just the last few minutes of the conversation, but it seemed to have happened that two coworkers had been having an affair. They both were married, they both had children, and neither were in the best of shape... physically. She moved her head forward, wrinkled up her nose, and lowered her voice when she shared the juicy details of how they had been having sex in the office. They had just been caught that day. Seems while everyone went to lunch together, they had stayed back to work on a special project. At this point the speaker paused, rolled her eyes up to the left, and took a deep breath in as if to indicate that she were about to share something very important. She lifted a very handsome hand to her bushy red hair and scratched her scalp with a seductively red, sharply manicured fingernail.

What happened was that all the girls who ordered their lunches to go had returned at the same time to eat in and help the other two with their project. A kind of "working lunch". What they found instead was the "fleshier" girl sitting on the desk with her pants off and her legs spread. There, between her soft billowy thighs, was the other woman. "A *different* kind of 'working lunch." It turned out that everybody was gonna be okay with it, except for maybe the husbands, but no-one was going to lose their job over it.

That was interesting and all, but I was the only guy in the room and felt a little uncomfortable as to where the conversation was going. But it *was* interesting. I moved out of the kitchen before it came around to the point in the conversation where I needed to share my part to keep the natural flow, grabbed myself a vodka and tonic at the bar, and moved out onto the patio.

Out on the patio is where the rowdier crowd was hanging out. They seemed to all be ahead of everyone else in the drink department. A little lewder; a little louder. This is where the smokers were, at least the social smokers, and the conversation was more like a middle eastern market. Open discussion; anyone, and sometimes everyone, would chime in at the same time. There were a lot of conversations going on. It sounded more like a busy bar than the rest of the party.

I grabbed a vacant lawn chair and sat at the periphery to take it in and see where I might interject myself. It was dark out here, with only orange jalapeño Christmas lights around the patio cover and over the top of the table, the hub of the conversation. A lot of the people were just silhouettes with voices. Some faces I only saw well as they held a lighter to the end of a cigarette and inhaled, stylishly exhaling that first lung full. There was one girl with longer hair and a band around her head like an Indian. She was athletic and attractive, but she was well on her way to being drunk, which made her seem silly and not as intelligent as she probably really was. She seemed to be having an unspoken competition to be louder and maybe drunker than a young man who also was athletic and attractive, but drinking, obviously. I thought to myself that they were in some kind of mating dance and, before the night was through, would be hooking up. That's just what I thought.

There was an Asian man (probably Cantonese) wearing a baseball cap. He was talking to someone, but I wasn't sure quite who. He looked ahead and a little to his left. I followed his line of sight. In that area was a woman with straight brown hair, soft features, and almost imperceptibly light freckles on her nose. She was wearing a soft black sweater that stood in contrast to her pale complexion. She was looking to the side and having a light conversation with the woman who sat to her immediate right. I could not hear a word as they spoke softly to one another, but they were both smiling. She was either purposely ignoring the Asian man, or was unaware that he was speaking in her direction.

Suddenly the girl with the head band bolted straight up. She raised her finger, pointing to the sky as if to call to everyone's attention that she was about to make an announcement. Everyone stopped mid-sentence and watched as she seemed to pause to gather her thoughts. She opened her mouth to speak and a column of puke sprung out of her. It erupted like a springy snake out of a peanut can -we're talking full-on fire hose. The column nose-dived to the wooden patio table and shattered into a thousand rivulets of shrapnel. Everyone, in unison, gasped abruptly and pushed away from the table. Most guests were spared, some were not, but the young attractive (and did I mention shirtless?) man with whom she was flirting took the brunt of the cascade. He stood up, backing away, arms spread, dripping... sticky.

"Oh my God!" he half-shouted, half-cried. Then he puked, too. Our host appeared bearing a towel and some cleaning supplies.

"Everyone go inside," she said calmly. "These guys got started early... they're amateurs, obviously." She smirked. She had a sense of humor about her. "I'm gonna call them a cab. Each. What they do when they leave here is not my business!" With that, everyone let out a collective laugh, except for the party pukers, who looked at the ground in shame, and the party continued. I was the last to go back, so I asked our hostess if she needed help with anything.

"No. I got it... this is my sister and her 'best friend' from childhood. They've always been like this. I wish they would just get it on and be done with it. " She laughed to herself, as if remembering something funny. "Really. I got it. I'll be just a minute with them. I'll see you inside."

I turned and went inside. *I hadn't noticed how delicate and caring her smile was.*

News of what had just happened was spreading inside the house. People were laughing and some were just in disgusted disbelief. Everyone shared their account of what just happened with those who had not yet heard and those who couldn't help but hear it again out of morbid curiosity. This disrupted the party and mixed things up a little. People were moving around, getting a fresh drink, mingling. I grabbed another vodka and tonic at the bar and went into the living room. This is where most of the party was seeming to settle back in. Even though the room was spacious, it was a little packed in, but not uncomfortable.

There was a woman in the corner of the room that I had not noticed before. She held my attention. She was wearing a black fedora-type hat. Her hair was shoulder length and platinum blonde, the whitest of white. Her skin was like porcelain. She wore dark sunglasses and her lips were bright red. She was wearing a gray smoking jacket with black velvet trim and sitting on a stool with her knees close together, her left hand on her bare thigh. In her right hand was a drink that she held delicately at about breast level; she would sip occasionally and daintily on the straw which stuck out of the glass. She was among a group of people, but no-one was talking to her and she wasn't talking. In fact, it seemed as if she were in a world all to herself behind those impenetrable dark sunglasses.

The party went on, as parties do. The night drew long and the drinks were flowing. I began to notice that there was a strange light in the room. In fact, my eyes were feeling rather dry and I felt it was this light that was making them burn. There was a couple standing next to me who were also observing the party and the story telling as it rotated around the room.

"Are your eyes burning?" I asked the thin, tall, man.

"Yeah, a little." he returned, leaning in and trying to keep his voice low. "There's a weird light in here. It's making it hard to focus."

"I noticed that, too," added his date, lowering a wine glass from her lips. She was unusually tall for a woman. She was thin, rail thin, and wearing a sleeveless black tube dress that nicely accented her small breasts and thin, lightly hairy arms. Her hair was cut in a bob and her eye makeup was heavy. She folded her arm across her body and rested her other elbow on it for support as she dangled the wine loosely by the stem. "Where's that light coming from?" She lifted the now empty wine glass. "Honey?"

"Gladly." He politely took the glass from her hand and walked to the bar.

"What do you think about that girl in the corner?" she said, turning her body toward me.

"I don't know," I said.

"Well… I think she's kind of hot. Don't you?"

"Yeah, I guess."

"I like to be with women," she confessed. "My husband and I are swingers."

"Great. I mean, that's awesome," I said, not knowing how to measure her statements.

She smiled and raised her eyebrow at me. I just looked back at her, our eyes locked. She leaned forward and kissed me. She stuck her tongue in my mouth, then leaned back and wiped her mouth with her forearm.

"I'll eat you up," she said.

"Hey, what's going on over here? Honey?" her husband asked nervously. He was holding two wine glasses. She grabbed the one out of his left hand and took a sip, looking down the glass at her husband as she drank.

"I'm going to the ladies' room," she announced and walked off, looking back at the two of us.

"Man, I'm sorry," he said sheepishly, drinking from his glass. "She gets this way sometimes. I guess she's had a little 'too much' tonight."

"Yeah." I didn't know what to do with my hands and they felt out of place just hanging there dumbly at my side.

"Did she tell you we were swingers or something?" he asked, nodding his head.

"Uh. Yeah."

"I know it wasn't you, so no hard feelings or anything. I guess she has this fantasy of being a swinger or something. She only does it when she's drunk. This isn't the first time. Sorry if she made you uncomfortable or gave you the wrong idea."

"No, no," I insisted by gesturing with both of my hands. I was uncomfortable, shocked, and feeling a little full of myself too. I had not planned on getting any unwarranted action, nor had a woman ever been so forward with me. *I must have had an effect on her, or maybe she was just drunk. Doesn't matter.* We just kind of stood there staring at each other. I didn't know what else to say.

"Cool?"

"Cool." I lifted my glass and walked over closer to the fireplace. I found myself strangely attracted to the woman, who, frankly, seemed out of place. She had an air of mystery about her. She sat there sipping a drink, yet never really acknowledging or participating in the party. I felt compelled to get closer to her. I moved closer, but not too close. I didn't want to seem like I was on the prowl or directly getting closer to her.

I stood there on the periphery of this smaller group of people. They seemed stiff and self-important. I wasn't really paying attention either. The guy in the suit and the turtle neck was still holding the attention of the group. I was beginning to dislike him; he was an alpha male wannabe. He kept his head, which seemed disproportionately large for his body, very straight as he spoke, and he spoke with the body language of authority, enunciating his speech almost with an accent, as if he were a member of some aristocracy. He was bragging. Boring. The other people were just standing around nodding. They were his entourage, his "yes men". I realized that, when it was convenient, he would mention "my book".

"Well, I was telling Dr. Morneux that I could have used that study for my book, but that I didn't agree with the method of the clinical trials,"or, "When I was in Monaco doing research for 'my book', I had the most delicate crab cakes at this little sidewalk cafe."

I could feel my resentment for him building as he droned on. I felt the blood pulsing in my face and neck. My eyes were burning from the strange light. I suddenly felt like the odd man out; I was hot and uncomfortable. I felt like I was being watched.

Scanning the room with my eyes, I lifted the drink to my lips. I noticed that the woman with the glasses had shifted her head and it seemed like she could be watching me by the tilt of her head, but it was difficult to determine. *What is her deal? I have to know.* I maintained an awareness of her with my peripheral vision. I took another sip of the drink and nodded in her direction to see if she would acknowledge me. I was pretending that my attempt at eye contact was incidental. She did not reciprocate my nod, as she sat there like a mannequin. I wanted to move closer to her, but I was playing a cat and mouse game; trying not to seem obvious.

Suddenly, and surprisingly, the porcelain blonde stood. Some guests took notice, including the big talker, and shifted their attention to her. Other guests, unaware of the unfolding situation, continued with their conversations. The magnetic effect of the woman on those who noticed was spellbinding and they stood in silence. She stripped off her smoking jacket and it dropped, as velvet, to the floor. Her movements were loaded with intent and she held her body in a way that spoke of her power. She was naked before us. Hands on hips, red lips pressed with mischievous tone. Others took notice as a hush fell upon the party. All eyes and attention were turning to the toned, athletic, yet soft statue that stood before us, wearing only a fedora and dark thick framed sunglasses. The curves of her body were defined and emphasized by her posture. The gravity was corporeal and the charge was building. There was a profound silence.

Without explanation and with no amount of courtesy, the big talker cleared his throat and announced, "As I was saying, in my book I was trying to communicate the dire consequences of the trajectory of, dare I say, the psychology and the terminology..."

He was cut short. The woman mechanically, almost diabolically, whipped her focus to him. She, with blinding swiftness, reached to her hat and flung it at the man, hitting him on the temple. The precision and the accuracy, in and of itself, was startling and impressive. The big talker flinched, raised his arms, and shrieked effeminately.

"I BEG YOUR PARDON!" he charged, his ego and self-importance highly challenged. "What the hell are you doing? Crazy bitch." He was straightening his jacket, his hair, and trying to regain his appearances. Everyone was watching. The woman stood motionless.

Her head was cocked to the right, her elbows by her sides, shrugging as if to state, "C'mon. What else have you got?".

"What the hell are you doing? You've got everyone's attention, that's what you want. So do your thing. Let's go. Otherwise, stop wasting our time." He scowled indignantly, shook his gelled spiky hair, and swept it back on the right side.

"As I was saying…" he started back into his conversation.

Suddenly, out of nowhere, loud aboriginal drumming began in the room. It was music intended to create a trance state. It was loud. It was mesmerizing and beautiful, yet intricately simple. She outstretched her arms, hands held in a delicate feminine way. Her body language was welcoming, suggestive, vulnerable. She began to undulate her hips. Each person in the room could feel her gaze emanate through the glasses. She was seducing us and drawing us into her sensuality. She moved like a flame before us. The whole party, including the big talker, stood mouth agape. She turned to us, bent over, and moved her hips. She ran her hands up her legs and rounded the curve of her hips, to her breasts, and over her head. Suddenly came the chiming of a crystal bowl, powerful, amplified, and seeming to come from everywhere. Everything in the room pulsed with its frequency. I could feel the sound deep inside my chest and in the floor.

She faced us all and peered at us from behind the glasses. She grabbed the side of the frames and paused, delicately. She removed the glasses. Immediately, the room was filled with a blinding, brilliant light. Our shadows stretched out behind us and retreated from its brilliance. Two beams of light blazed out of the orifices where her eyes should be. They peered out at each of us as she swept the room with her gaze, seeming to burn right through us. Everyone stood frozen in terror. No-one moved. We stood like terrified corpses before her, limp and asleep, eyes transfixed.

Light flowed out from behind; she stood in a full body halo. She opened her mouth wide and a column of light burst forth with the opening of her jaw. Her hands were held down, palms facing us. She levitated off the floor. As she floated before us, she began to rotate to the left.

"I am Shakti," she said with a voice that came from the center of *my* skull and echoed into the room. "Each of you will experience me in a different way. Some will have no memory of me at all." Her mouth did not move.

The light was blinding and my eyes involuntarily rolled up in my head and I struggled to keep them open. She turned like a menacing light house, as the beams coming from her eyes and mouth scanned the room. She rotated faster and faster, the room strobing in a contrast of twilight and noon.

In one instance, the entire room was entangled in a writhing mass of bodies and love making. In another instant, she was holding me in her arms as I lay with my head between her breasts. I watched as she had sex with numerous men and women, sometimes individually, sometimes exclusively. There was dancing, music, and lights. She was the light that made it possible to see as she hung there in the middle of the room, simultaneously in the mass of bodies with us. Sometimes she held me in the light and I cried. Others too had sobbing attacks out of sheer tantric joy. The room faded away from me and I was alone in a cloud of white. Out of the light walked the woman in a white robe. Her hair was long and brown and fell upon her shoulders in ringlets, but it was her. I knew as she approached me.

"I've been waiting for you, Lover. It has been a long time, hasn't it?" She smiled lovingly.

I felt warm and familiar and loved. I had known her before in a sunny spot, on green, cool grass by the ocean. *When?*

"What's going on?" I asked.

"You don't remember?"

"Yes, I do, but..."

"Time is a limited idea. We *forget* to relieve the pain of separation. The pain of loneliness."

"I don't..."

"We are never alone; we are always together. I love you."

I wept. My body shuddered as I stood there. It started to rain. My heart was breaking a thousand times.

"You don't remember," she said, lowering her head. She looked up at me and a tear ran down her cheek. "You don't remember!" she shoved me in the chest with both hands. "You don't fucking remember. You asshole!" she was screaming now, enraged. She changed into a huge tigress and lay outstretched before me. There was a yellow light that emanated from behind her.

I stood terrified, in a sphere of yellow with nowhere to go; just me, the tiger, and encapsulating darkness.

"What do you want from me?" I cried.

"I want you to remember." The tiger sat there. I could see her body moving with each quickening breath. The head and nose wrinkled as she turned to peer at me with predator eyes and a growl. A spiritual terror seized my body. Frozen, I crossed my arms and put my hands on my shoulders as I cried.

"I want to remember. I want to remember!" I cried.

There was a moment of eye contact between me and the tiger. She looked through me. She looked into my soul. Her body tensed.

"Please. Don't." I groveled.

She uncoiled at me with ferocious speed. I covered my face as she came upon me, right paw raised. I could see the black razor-sharp claws extended. She swung at me.

I woke up with a start as I gasped for breath. In a puddle of sweat, I didn't immediately know where I was. I raised my head and looked around. I was still at the house of the party, in the living room where I last remembered standing. The other party goers were scattered around. Everyone was asleep. I pushed my torso off the floor with heavy arms and sat up. I shook my head in remembrance of what had taken place. *Where was she?* I scanned the room but did not see her. I noticed the thin woman who had been so forward and had kissed me. She was lying on the floor with her back to me, her legs curled up in a fetal position. Her dress was pulled up just enough to reveal a pair of red panties and just the bottom curve of her buttocks. Her hands were clasped beneath her head. *How peaceful she looks,* I thought. Asleep, she seemed more attractive to me. Her husband was laying on the other side of the room against a wall, sprawled out on his back and snoring. Other party members were lying about the room and in the adjacent rooms. On the couch, I noticed the big talker curled up with a throw pillow, sucking his thumb. I recognized the hostess asleep in a big reclining chair, empty wine glass in her hand, head cocked back, mouth open, eyes closed. *How would she explain the events of the night?* There was no sign of what I had envisioned; no-one was naked. Everybody seemed to have passed out in their respective spots and all of the furniture seemed to be in place. I got up as quietly as possible without waking anyone. I tip-toed out the front door and quietly closed it behind me. I walked to my car which was parked on the street. It was an unusually bright, humid morning. I started my car and drove off to find the closest cup of coffee.

# The Documentary

"That really stinks," came a voice from somewhere behind me. The three of us were startled at the timely delivery of the criticism.

"Could you put a bit more of yourself into that? Where are you, at a high school play? You couldn't have possibly over-acted that more. Loosen up."

"Who is *that?*" Betty asked in a high, nasal, Texas drawl.

We came to the woods to film a scene. As an actor *and* the director, I was so focused on delivering my lines and setting up the scene that it hadn't occurred to me that someone was watching. The voice had pulled me out of character and brought me crisply into the moment. I was trying to figure out where I had heard it before. I looked at Betty, I looked at Rob. He pulled his eye away from the camera's eye piece , looked at me, shrugged, and continued filming.

"That criticism was spot on, but kinda harsh, don't ya think?" I asked in no specific direction.

"Yes, but you would assume that a beauty such as this would have more acting ability in her somewhere."

Betty was incensed. She was physically beautiful and, much to the tribulation of her admirers, had taken a vow of chastity before marriage, not even a kiss. She was outspoken, especially in regard to her beliefs. Her wit and an enduring naïve quality made her all the more attractive. She was about to respond when Rob interrupted her.

"James Dean," he blurted. He dropped his camera for a second and snapped his fingers at me. "It's James Dean," he repeated.

"Don't be silly, but he was a fine actor. Wouldn't you say?" said the voice.

"Why don't you come out and work with us?  I could use some help with this scene,"  I asked.

"Sure, but are you ready?"

"Ready for what?"

"For this?"

There was a flash of movement, a rustling in the tall grass, and out of the brush came a *chimpanzee* wearing only a black cotton T-shirt. He cocked his head to one side and, like a scene from "Rebel Without a Cause", reached into his front pocket, pulled out a cigarette, tapped the end on his wrist, raised it to his mouth, and lit it with a zippo lighter. He inhaled deeply and exhaled, creating a cloud about his face.

"Are you surprised?" He grinned.

Everything within my being was urging me to turn and run. My knees were shaking and my heart was trying to leap from my chest. This did not fit within the boundaries of what my mind accepted as reality. I thought I might faint.

"Don't stare. It's not polite." He took another drag off the cigarette and exhaled a lungful of smoke. His movements were animated; he embodied his words as he spoke. "How do you prepare for something like this? Would you have believed me if I had told you I was a 'monkey'? You wouldn't, and you would have been just as shocked when you saw me. No, I think it is best to *jump in* when the water is cold. At first, the shock is overwhelming, but it wears off a bit sooner." The way he held his jaw gave him a dignified air. My senses were returning. Rob and Betty, still in utter disbelief, were trying to process what was happening.

"Now, little miss thang you have out here in the woods; I'm hoping this is going to turn into a nude scene." He took another drag and winked at Betty.

"I'm not that kind of girl," she said. "Rude."

"I'm a male. If you haven't noticed," he motioned toward his genitals. "There aren't any females out here, if you know what I mean."

"Eww. Why aren't you wearing pants?" Betty was shaking the visual from her head. "Why are you here?" she asked.

"Hold on there, Tex," he mimicked Betty's accent. "Let me level with you." He took another drag on his cigarette and paused. His body language changed; he was thinking. He looked at the ground. "Not too far from here is an experimental laboratory. You don't know about it because it is not one of those places that advertises. It's funded by the government and manned by military personnel. I live there." He looked up at us. "I'm part of an experiment to develop the mental capabilities of soldiers so they perform better on the battlefield. They use chimpanzees because of the genetic similarity to humans. I learned to speak, as well as do a lot of other 'human' things." He made quotation marks with his hands again and winked at Betty. "I was injected with human DNA as a fetus, so technically I'm part human. Jack is the weekend and night guard - also my closest friend. We play chess together, watch movies, get drunk. We have a deal. I let him sleep while I watch the other animals and do the paperwork, he lets me come outside."

"But there's nothing out here but trees and animals. Why would you want to be out here?" Betty asked.

"For the same reason I am not wearing any pants, girlfriend. I'm a monkey." His delivery broke the ice and we all laughed; a bond was forming.

"I come out here because I'm a chimp and I love being in the forest. Because I'm human, I love my freedom and don't want to be locked up. Sometimes I like to be alone with my thoughts." He looked at Rob, then me, raised his fist to his crotch, and made several stroking motions.

"Would you stop with the vulgar, sexual references? It's offensive. What they're doing out here is wrong. They are playing God." Betty was speaking her mind.

"Betty? Is that your name? I'll tone it down. I haven't been around many women, so I'm having a hard time controlling my hormones. Seriously, you don't...? You know," he shrugged "I just can't believe it. Look at you. What a waste."

Betty crossed her arms in front of her chest.

"I suppose that you don't believe that humans evolved from... well... a chimpanzee."

"No, I don't." she stated.

"I guess you buy that whole Adam and Eve thing?"

She put one hand on her hip and raised the other to help her make a point. He interrupted her.

"Look, Betty, I think we're getting off on the wrong foot here. You obviously don't believe in evolution, so let's just agree to disagree. Okay?"

I could sense Betty's frustration. Having known her since Kindergarten, I knew this was about to get ugly... fast.

"Everyone calls me Jim." He took the last drag of his cigarette and pitched the butt onto the ground, crushing it with his foot.

"Jim…" I extended my hand to him. "Did you say there's an experimental lab near here?" We shook hands. His smile was warm and his eyes were kind. He shook hands with Rob and Betty. She looked appalled but, knowing her like I did, I could tell that she was warming up.

"It's about four miles from here." He offered to take us there. We all agreed and followed him. He told us what growing up was like - his earliest interaction was with humans. Through constant testing and examinations, he learned early on that he was different. Although human on the inside, he looked like a chimpanzee. Ten years ago, Jack had been assigned to weekend and night duty. Jack was really good for him. He had taught him about the world, sports, women, art, and acting. He was a refined man and a good role model for Jim. It turns out that Jack and, likewise, Jim had excellent taste in movies. Jim really enjoyed John Wayne, Marlon Brando, and James Dean movies; he had a keen acting sense and could embody the characters he was exposed to. He suddenly stopped dead in his tracks and began to whisper.

"We're about 500 yards from the facility. Since you're here, I wonder if you would be interested in coming inside and shooting a documentary about what's going on here. Jack and I have talked about doing a piece to blow the cover off of this place. I'm treated well, but this is a prison.  My story has a wide range of appeal. It would be an inspirational, cross-cultural, high concept message with a far-reaching effect. There's the religious aspect - it questions what is humanity and human consciousness? Is it possible for me to assimilate into society? Do I have legal rights? What do you think? It's no accident that we ran into each other in the woods. We just have to get you past Zeke."

"Who's Zeke?" Rob asked changing the camera angle.

"Zeke guards the outer perimeter and takes his job too seriously. We used to hang out, but he got into trouble and was almost re-assigned to Alaska. He and Jack brought a stripper here for my 21st birthday. I had never seen a woman naked in real life. She was doing her thing and the chimpanzee in me got out of control. I started humping on her leg. I guess she wasn't feeling the love, left in a huff, and called the authorities.  The Sheriff showed up and wanted to know what was going on. Zeke stalled them at the gate, but there was an investigation. Management was alerted to the breech of security and it fell on Zeke's watch. He's never gotten over it. So, are you on board?"

We all nodded.

"Great. Let me talk to Jack. You guys stay here. If I'm not back in an hour, come back tomorrow around this time." He turned and disappeared into the trees.

"This is awesome, dude. We're about to sneak into a secret laboratory and film a talking monkey. Rob finally took a break from filming. "We have at least an hour of amazing footage. This is incredible."

"I was thinking the same thing. This could be our life's work."

"This is like getting to film at Area 51. We're going *inside*," Rob liked the direction this was going.

Betty said, "I still think it's wrong, but I'm game - only to help Jim out."

"I thought you didn't like him," I whispered.

"He's starting to grow on me."

"Betty, you sound like you're falling for him." I half joked.

"NO! He's too short, and hairy," she shook her head.

Thirty minutes later, Jim reappeared. The plan was to shoot Zeke with a tranquilizer dart when he came out for his next patrol with enough of a dose to keep him out for six hours. Once he was unconscious, Jim would adjust the surveillance cameras to create a blind spot. Betty, Rob, and I would enter and exit the facility through this blind spot. We would go to Jim's living area, film the interview, and get footage of how he lived. Jack and Jim would sit Zeke at the desk as if he had fallen asleep on the job. He would be too afraid to say anything. Zeke would wake up groggy, but just in time to finish his paperwork before the day crew arrived. Jack was already in position to make the shot.

At 7:05 pm, Zeke stepped out the door of the guard shack. He stretched and adjusted his pistol holster as he stepped off the curb. There was the small pop of the air rifle and a faint hiss as the dart struck its mark.

"What the...?" Zeke pulled at the dart that pierced his buttock, but it was too late. Unconsciousness was closing in on him. He gently dropped to one knee, then rolled over and was out. Jim adjusted the cameras and gave the thumbs up to Jack, who came out of hiding.

"He's out like a light. Let's get him in the guard shack." Jack was all business.

They lifted his body and gently placed him in the chair, his feet propped up on the desk. They motioned for the others to come on in. Rob was first, then Betty, then me. As we passed the guard shack, Zeke clamored out the door.

"Hey... you guys can't come in here. You need a security code..." he was slurring his speech and trailing off. He looked at Jack. "What's going on here? You're gonna get us fired."

"Well hello!" Betty spoke loudly and sweetly. She was walking toward Zeke and unbuttoning the top of her blouse. Zeke just smiled dopily. "Is today your birthday, sailor? 'Cause I feel like having a party. Let's get you back inside." This was totally out of character for her. She slinked over and took him by the arm. He followed her like a puppy into the guard shack. She sat him in the chair and began a slow striptease. His eyes soon rolled back in his head and his mouth fell open. He snored.

"I sure hope you don't have that effect on all men, sweetheart," Jim piped up from the corner of the room. "That was some good thinking. Let's pull his pants down so when he wakes up he thinks something happened. You know," he made a suggestive gesture.

"Oh, you are good," Betty answered, "really good."

"We've got to get moving," Jack said, taking charge. "This is our chance to get Jim's story out." We took a short tour as we filmed. The base was relatively small, maybe 30 acres surrounded by a high fence with Concertina wire and electricity. In decades past it was used for different purposes, being largely hidden and surrounded by miles of national forest, with only one nondescript and seldom traveled road in or out. There was a central building, single floor office, nothing exceptional, with several smaller annex buildings, a garage/shop area, and a few military trucks and vehicles. There were several hangars, a runway, a sports field, and a helicopter pad. It had the appearance of a small airport that said "nothing to see here".

In the main building were several rooms with computers and lab equipment. Another room has walls lined with cages that housed small animals, such as rats and rabbits. There were beakers, racks of tubes, petri dishes, and microscopes.

There was a kitchen and dining area large enough to feed a small staff of people. A media room with a dated projector, TV, and shelves of books and movies, alongside couches for reading and viewing. It was nothing fancy, but it was what you might expect of a ward where people were due to stay long-term. Everything had the air of previous decades' use.

Jim had his own room, with a bed and closet for his clothes. However, no matter how comfortable the accommodations, this was still a prison for one.

Jack sat in his favorite movie-watching chair as we filmed his interview. He was comfortable and confident. We promptly packed our gear and left when we finished. Jim's story touched us all. After everything he had been through he was neither bitter nor angry. Four months and many hours at the editing desk later, we had a film we could be proud of. We released trailers on the internet and held independent theater openings all over the country. People were moved by Jim's story. It garnered enough attention that the lab was closed down. Jack retired from the military and was granted custody of Jim. They both earned enough money from speaking engagements and appearances that they have now moved to Costa Rica. They live the life they always dreamed of, surrounded by pristine nature and, occasionally, a beautiful woman.